The
Raven
Queen

che golden

The
Raven
Queen

Quercus

New York • London

Quercus

New York • London

© 2013 by Che Golden
First published in the United States by Quercus in 2015

ISBN 978-1-62365-635-5

Library of Congress Control Number: 2015946254

Distributed in the United States and Canada by
Hachette Book Group
1290 Avenue of the Americas
New York, NY 10104

Manufactured in the United States

10 9 8 7 6 5 4 3 2 1

www.quercus.com

Even darkness must pass

J.R.R. TOLKIEN

A NOTE FROM THE AUTHOR

In this book, some of the characters have unusual names. To find out how to say them, turn to pages 251.

Prologue

The black wolf felt the hair on his back rise with fear. He shook his head, his thick black ruff of fur rippling on his neck. He had been summoned by the Winter Queen and that couldn't be good, whatever mood Queen Liadan was in. Fenris found it best if no one noticed him or his pack in Tír na nÓg. He was sure that if Queen Liadan had not extended her protection over the pack, there were plenty of faeries that would enjoy a wolf hunt. Fenris had made sure the other wolves, especially Nitania and her cubs, were hidden deep in the brooding forest of Tír na nÓg before he set off for the White Tower.

He was no coward, but it had been very hard to place one paw in front of another as he had crossed the ice bridge that Liadan had sculpted from the waters of the lake with her cold touch. The bridge arched to the foot of a crumbling road that led to the copper gates barring the way to the Winter Court's stronghold. The gates swung open silently at his approach. All was still and quiet as he padded along the road, with only his shadow and the sound of his breathing to keep him company. In the rest of Tír na nÓg, spring was giving way to summer. Queen Sorcha of the Spring Court would be weeping and tearing at her hair as the power of the season ebbed from her court, while Queen Niamh of Summer would be gloating in triumph as she felt her strength grow. Queen Liadan brooded while waiting for the earth to turn to winter, and while she brooded, winter's cold leaked from her.

Outside the White Tower the air was balmy. The placid waters of the lake sparkled like diamonds in the afternoon sunshine and the ice bridge wept in the heat. But within the White Tower winter reigned and hoar frost shone on every inch of stone. Fenris's breath curled from his mouth and formed droplets on his whiskers. The tower reached into the sky above him, twisting and turning on itself as it climbed. So high did it reach, so narrow were its uppermost turrets, that the courtyard at its base would have been shrouded in eternal darkness had Liadan not created a staircase of mirrors to catch the sunlight. The light stepped all the way down the stone frills of the balconies and windows, through the ruined fortress that only ghosts now called home, all the way down to Liadan's hall, where she trapped it.

The hall sat neat and simple in the chaos of the overblown tower, testament to the taste and modesty of a past Winter Queen. Rippling stone steps led to massive double wooden doors carved with flowers and beasts. Ice crackled over their surface, silvering a wood that had been blackened with age. Frost crept beneath them and inched its way down the steps with slow-moving fingers. Fenris shuddered. The Winter Queen was angry.

The ice burned the rough pads of his paws and he flinched as he made his painful way up the steps to stand outside the doors. The golden lock, crafted by a smith who was long since dust and bones, began to click and whirr at his approach before springing open, letting the doors swing wide enough for him to slip his lean body between them.

The court was full. Every faerie that served Liadan was present in all its finery. Golden sunlight lit up diamonds, emeralds, rubies, and sapphires, sleek inhuman hair, the soft pelts of the furs the faeries wore as protection against their own queen's cold. All eyes turned to Fenris as he padded into the hall, but no one spoke. The building pulsed to the rhythm of a crowd breathing, but not a cough nor a sigh disturbed the eerie silence. Thick, soft rugs lay beneath the feet of the courtiers as they watched him from behind fluted columns that lined a path to the glittering throne of crystal where Queen Liadan sat. Fenris held his head high as he walked slowly toward the Winter Queen. He did not need to turn his head to see her court. No Tuatha graced her hall, only golden, glittering elves with their beautiful cold faces and their diamond-bright eyes. Standing among them were the plainer, darker shapes of sprites, trolls, goblins, gancanagh, glaistigs, and other faeries who were drawn to the cruelty and madness of Liadan's rule for the blood and the fear and the pain they feasted on. Fenris was surrounded by enemies who would rip him apart in seconds, but he gritted his teeth and focused on the tiny figure seated in front of him.

She was dressed in a simple white gown, her hair hanging straight and heavy, so long she could sit on it. Black as a raven's wing, it framed the stark bones of her snow-white face. Her eyes had been boiled white by the cold that had consumed her when the Winter crown had been placed upon her head. It had killed the color in her face so that now her blood-red lips were painted on, and the roses in her cheeks had withered to gray.

"You disappoint me, Fenris," said Liadan. Powdered ice puffed from her painted lips with every breath. Ice crept from her feet and began to inch toward him, spreading thin fingers as it came.

"I am sorry for it, Highness," said Fenris.

"No, I think not," said Liadan. "To say you are sorry means you regret what you did and implies you would never do it again. And yet, despite my displeasure, you have twice helped the Feral Child."

Fenris said nothing, merely blinked his long eyes slowly.

Liadan tipped her head to one side. "Do you know why I named you Fenris, when I found your pack staggering through Tír na nÓg, terrified and bewildered? Fenris, according to my people, was a wolf who would eat the moon at the end of days and bring about the destruction of the world. You, Fenris, seem to be determined to bring about the destruction of *my* world. But I know how to deal with you, wolf."

The wolf tensed and his ears swiveled back as he caught the sounds of soft footsteps creeping up behind him and the slither of a chain running between fingers. He whipped around, ears pinned to his head, and snarled in the faces of the three faeries who held a long silver chain between them. He crouched to spring, but as he launched himself into the air they rushed at him, lifting the chain high so that it passed between his snapping teeth, and as it caught the corners of his mouth the impact threw him to the ground. The breath whooshed from his lungs and he heard a crack as one of his ribs broke against the flagstone floor. His attackers were on him in seconds, winding the chain around his muzzle to keep them safe from his teeth and then binding his legs with the cold, slippery silver. He kicked and struggled and scraped long claw marks in the stone with his black nails, but it was no use. The giggling faeries pressed him down with knees and hands and one grabbed the chain around his muzzle and yanked hard on it, twisting his head up so he had to look directly at the red-eyed faerie who stood over him. Her bone-white skin crawled with gray tattoos and her ice-white hair was stiffened with lime so it swept up and away from her pointed face in a Mohican. Fenris's eyes bulged as she began to draw her sword.

"Your namesake was bound, just like this, and his jaws were pinned with a sword to stop him biting," said Liadan. "They say he is tied to a rock beneath the earth, waiting for the time of chaos. He is strong, Fenris, stronger than you, but how he must suffer. Your suffering will be much greater and I think it will bring your little friend running. Let's see how long the Feral Child can ignore the cries of her friends as they pay for her arrogance, before she tries to save them."

Terrified, Fenris bucked and heaved to get the faeries off him as the red-eyed creature lifted the sword with the hilt clasped in both hands, but they simply laughed and pinned his head and legs to the ground. His panicked breath rasped between his teeth and a keen of pure fear vibrated in his throat. He closed his eyes as he felt the tip of the blade prick the soft flesh under his jaw. His howl of pain was strangled as the blade lunged upward, pinning his tongue. Blood filled his mouth, and as the faeries lowered his now limp head to the floor it pooled beneath his face, warm and sticky in the ice-cold hall. As he shuddered with shock he was dimly aware of the light laughter of the court and Liadan's voice saying, "Look, Fachtna, wolf tears. Collect them for me, would you? I imagine they are quite rare."

chapter one

MADDY SQUINTED INTO THE HAZY SUMMER SUN-
shine and sighed. She hated duty visits and hated especially coming to visit Great-Aunt Kitty, who lived in a
nursing home on the outskirts of the suburbs of Cork
city. For Maddy, these visits were particularly uncom-
fortable, as she knew she could end up here herself. The
problem was that Great-Aunt Kitty had been driven
insane by the Sight. A lot of the people in the home would
have lived normal, happy lives if their ability to see faeries had not gotten them tangled up with the inhabit-
ants of Tír na nÓg. But many of them had tried to warn
people of the malevolent creatures that moved among
them and they had been laughed at, mocked, and eventually locked away when their families and communi-
ties decided they were crazy. Maddy could look around

the garden of this place and see her future. Great-Aunt Kitty probably had gone a little bit senile with old age, but once she had been just like Maddy. It did not help to watch Una, the family banshee, wandering around the Victorian walled garden saying hello to everyone, like a guest at a school reunion. Maddy noticed the white-uniformed nurses frowning at the patients, who looked as if they were talking to thin air.

You're not helping, Una, thought Maddy. *If these people keep talking to faeries, they'll never get out of here.*

She looked at her great-aunt, who was smiling away at nothing in particular, her papery, wrinkled hands folded in her lap.

Maddy cleared her throat. "I'm sorry, Aunt Kitty, I have to go. I'll see you soon though."

The tiny woman smiled. "I know you do, Maddy. I can feel it."

Here we go, thought Maddy, as her blood ran cold. "Feel what?"

"There's a reckoning coming, blood and fire and ice, and the Hound will have to run," said Aunt Kitty. She turned her eyes on Maddy, her sweet smile still lingering on her lips. "But who will you run for?"

"What do you mean?" asked Maddy.

"We all know what you did," said Aunt Kitty, shaking her head ever so slightly. "So we don't know who the Hound will run for—us or the red-haired queen?"

"Us," said Maddy. "Mortals, always. How could you think any different?"

"Because you made a bargain, girl," said Aunt Kitty, the softness fleeing her face as her eyes turned cold. "You bent the knee and you swore an oath of fealty to a faerie. You have to keep your word, girl, always. What is a Hound without honor?"

"I always do the right thing," said Maddy.

"Do you now?" asked Aunt Kitty, leaning in close with such a cold expression that her silvery blue eyes darkened to steel. "Is it right, or is it what you think is right? Because that's a different thing altogether."

Maddy thought back to last year and the blood that had drenched the autumn grass. Innocent blood from a person she had unwittingly condemned to death, so sure was she that she was doing the right thing. The smell of autumn rain cut through the heavy scent of summer roses. She could hear the hiss of that long red hair as it trailed over plaid wool. *You thought you were* moral. *You thought you were* righteous. *How does it feel now, hero?* asked a voice in her head. She closed her eyes for a second and saw the light go out in an innocent's eyes and his last breath cool in his mouth.

Aunt Kitty watched her closely and then smiled, a humorless, cynical and very, very sane twist of the lips, before giving a brief nod and sitting back in her chair.

"I thought so," she said.

Maddy opened her mouth to defend herself, but the words choked in her throat. She stared at her great-aunt, who simply turned her face up to the sun, closed her eyes, and smiled again as its rays bathed her skin.

Una chose that moment to come strolling up with the awkward, rolling gait that made her rock from side to side as she walked. She looked a horror, with lank, gray hair so thin it showed her wrinkled scalp, long bare hands and feet that were filthy and tipped with black, horny nails. Her clothes, torn and tattered grave shrouds, were wound around her emaciated body. One tooth hung on gamely in her wrinkled, sagging mouth. But her eyes were warm and kind and full of laughter. If it were not for her eyes, Maddy would have run screaming at the sight of her. The little banshee was tied to Maddy's family. Every time one of them died she mourned with a loud keening that could be heard in both the mortal and the faerie worlds. She was a weird sort of guardian angel, but her magical ability to know where anyone in the family was at any time had come in very handy in the past. It was as though Una could track Maddy and anyone related to her with her own faerie GPS system. As long as she did not get distracted by Cheese & Onion Tayto crisps, for which she had a terrible weakness.

As it was, she had managed to beg a few sweets off the inmates and was loudly crunching them between her gums.

Maddy made a face. "Una, doesn't that hurt?"

The little banshee tapped her gums with the tip of a black fingernail. "Rock hard. Eating without teeth for two hundred years will do that to them." She leaned forward and touched Aunt Kitty lightly on the arm with her grubby fingertips. "How are you keeping, Kathleen?"

Aunt Kitty opened her eyes and beamed at the little banshee. "Good, thanks. Yourself?"

"Not so bad, hanging in there," said Una.

"You'll be around forever, you will," said Aunt Kitty. "How many of us have you watched over?"

"Oh, too many to count," said Una. "You're looking well yourself."

"Oh aye, I'm going dancing later on!" said Aunt Kitty.

The two of them laughed as Maddy rolled her eyes. "They have no idea how to enjoy themselves these days, do they, these young ones?" Aunt Kitty asked Una. "They drag themselves around the place, dressed in black like widow women, and listen to that awful music. You couldn't even sing to that nonsense, sure you couldn't."

Una chuckled and shook her head. "And they look at us old ones and think we never had fun. Sure, fun only came along when they invented it."

"Really?" Maddy asked Una. "When was the last time you went clubbing?"

Una glared at her. "Don't be smart, Madeline, it doesn't suit you."

Aunt Kitty gave a snort. "Do you remember the dances we had in town, Una? Do you remember that black net dress of mine, with the sticky-out skirt? I spent half a week's wages on sequins that I had to go all the way into town on the bus for, and nearly made myself blind sewing them all on. Mammy was scandalized. But, oh, how it sparkled! And Mammy gave me a loan of her lipstick, and Dermot said that when I danced I looked like I was made of stars."

"I remember, Kathleen," said Una. "You used to come home so flushed and happy, your eyes were the biggest stars of all."

"Do you ever see Dermot?"

Una frowned. "From time to time. He's well, if that's what you're asking."

"Who did he marry again?"

"Noreen O'Hara, the one that used to live out on the road to Mallow."

Aunt Kitty clicked her tongue. "I remember her. She used to chase after all the boys."

"Well, she caught up with Dermot right enough," said Una.

Aunt Kitty looked at Maddy. "He told me he would love me forever," she whispered, her voice full of unshed tears. "It turned out forever didn't last as long as I thought it would."

Pretty, witty Kitty, the baby of her family, whose wispy white hair was once thick brown curls. For a moment, Maddy saw the girl who danced for so long on a Saturday night she would have to ease her high heels from her aching feet and carry them, dangling from the tips of two fingers, as she walked home down the lane to the cottage in Blarney, the cold stone of the street pressing through her black seamed stockings. She saw her smile as she touched her lips, her dress of stars twinkling in the moonlight. Pretty, witty Kitty, her life ruined by the secrets in Blarney.

A nurse began to ring a bell to signal visiting time was over. Maddy jumped up and fussed with her bag, checking her phone and trying not to look too relieved. Una rolled her eyes, while Aunt Kitty cackled.

"Look at her," said Una. "I've seen greyhounds start a race slower."

Maddy hid her blush by bending her head right down to rummage in the bag. "Auntie Fionnula sent some stuff for you. I've got a box of those jellied fruits you like and a fruitcake . . ."

"I'll take the sweets but Fionnula can keep her cake," said Great-Aunt Kitty, making a sour face. "Never could bake, that one—her cakes are always dry. You couldn't even feed the ducks with them; poor things would sink, if you didn't brain them first, chucking the stuff at them."

With a sinking heart, Maddy looked down at the cookie tin that held Aunt Fionnula's cake. Great-Aunt Kitty had a point, but she could just see Aunt Fionnula's gimlet eyes narrowing with rage when Maddy brought it back. Somehow this was going to be her fault. Aunt Fionnula was, unjustifiably, very proud of her baking. This slur would not go unnoticed, no matter what excuse Maddy came up with.

"Are you sure?" she asked.

"Positive!" said Kitty. "I'm not as crazy as people think I am. I'd know if I wanted Fionnula's burned cakes stuck in my craw. But if there is anyone I want to finish off in here, I'll be sure to give you a call."

The banshee and the old woman hooted with laughter while Maddy stuffed the cake back into the bag. People were drifting toward the exit. "I really do actually have to go," she said.

"Off you trot then," said Kitty. "Don't let me keep you. But you can tell Fionnula that she can get off her backside and come herself next time."

I would have to be suicidal to do that, thought Maddy.

Kitty closed her eyes again and leaned her head back against the chair. Her face was sunken with age and the bones of her skull stood out sharply. Maddy hesitated, wondering if she should kiss her great-aunt good-bye. But as she stood there, dithering, Kitty put a hand out and clutched her wrist.

"You'll be fine, girl," she said, her eyes still closed against the summer sun. "You just need to know what the Hound knows."

"What is that then?"

Kitty pulled her hand away and tutted. "How should I know? Do I look like the Hound?"

Una plucked at Maddy's arm and nodded her head toward the exit. "We'll be off now, Kitty," she said. "I'll see you soon?"

"You will, please God," said Kitty, and then her head nodded onto her chest.

Una and Maddy left Kitty sleeping in her chair and made their way through the sun-drenched garden to the beautiful building that had once housed nuns. It took a second for Maddy's eyes to adjust to the dim light of the nursing home, and its cool air kissed her sunburnt arms. A grand wooden staircase and dark oak paneling gleamed in the half-light and gave off a faint whiff of beeswax polish. Maddy's sneakers squeaked on the elaborate tiled floor that led to stained-glass double doors. She noticed that even though no one around them gave any sign that they could see Una, the little faerie woman was given a wide berth—no one got close enough to jostle her or tread on her bare, dirty feet.

The small crowd of visitors spilled out into the parking lot. It could have been her imagination, but Maddy was sure the chattering voices were high with relief as they left their disturbed and disturbing relatives. Or perhaps it was her own guilt talking, because Maddy was certainly glad to escape poor Kitty.

She heaved the tote bag that Aunt Fionnula had insisted she bring with her onto her shoulder. It was too big for her skinny frame and the cookie tin banged against her hip with every step. No doubt the dry-as-dust cake was disintegrating with each bounce and it would just add to the trouble Maddy was in, but she was too hot to care. She dug into her jeans pocket for the cell phone Granda had insisted she have with her at all times and dialed Aunt Fionnula's number. After about three rings, she was relieved to hear Roisin pick up the phone. Relations were still strained between Maddy and Aunt Fionnula and the less she had to do with her aunt, the better.

"Ro, it's me. Can someone come get me? Visiting time is over. I'm in the parking lot." She heard Aunt Fionnula's sharp voice in the background and her name rapped out in short, hard notes. Roisin's voice dropped to a whisper.

"Um, Mom's a bit busy right now. She wants to know if you can walk back?"

"You are joking, right?" said Maddy. "I'm melting out here, and it's at least a half-hour walk back."

There was a scuffling noise as Aunt Fionnula grabbed the phone from Roisin. "Maddy, where are you?"

"The parking lot at the nursing home," said Maddy, through gritted teeth. "Waiting on a lift."

"Madeline, you know full well I don't have time to be running around after you!" barked Aunt Fionnula.

"But it's a really long walk . . ." began Maddy, but Aunt Fionnula cut her off.

"It's twenty minutes at the most, and you have young legs on you. The walk will do you good."

Maddy stared in disbelief as the phone went dead in her hand. *She hung up on me,* she thought, as she glared at the little screen. She stuck her tongue out at it. "Cow!" she hissed.

Una tutted, which just annoyed Maddy even more. She fished the cookie tin out of her bag, walked over to a nearby trashcan, flipped the lid and slid the cake into the trash.

"You are a wicked child," said Una, with a slight smile hovering at the edges of her wrinkled lips. "And you're not too old for a smack either."

Maddy grinned at her. "But you're far too short to give me one. What are you going to do, stand on a box?"

Una laughed and crouched down on the pavement, poking a long black nail into her mouth to pry a last piece of toffee off her hardened gums. She sighed. "It's a shame Fionnula has to be angry with you—it's fiercely hot. A lift would be nice."

It certainly was. It was one of the rare days in Cork when the heat was not tempered by a dewy breeze blowing straight in off the sea. The air was still and heavy and Maddy could feel her hair dampening at the nape of her neck. She rubbed at her face. She never really coped well with the heat and always seemed to get a mustache of grime as sweat collected around her lips.

She sighed and eased her thumb under the bag's shoulder strap. She really should have brought a bottle of water, but she did not think of it, and she had no money to buy one. Of course, she had thought she was going to be getting a lift home.

"C'mon, we might as well get walking," she said to the little banshee. "I'll probably cop an earful if she thinks I've been messing on the way."

But just as the words left her mouth, the blistering heat cooled, just a little, a tang of ozone tickled her nostrils and her sweat-wet hair rose on the nape of her neck. Maddy and Una stared at each other, their eyes widening in fear.

"Can you feel that too?" asked Maddy.

Una nodded and stood up, her eyes darting from side to side. "We have to get you out of here . . . we're too far from the city . . . we need to be surrounded by iron!"

"They can't get at me here. The city is only twenty minutes' walk away!" said Maddy.

"Too far, still too far. It won't stop a solitary, one of the older, stronger faeries; they can still get to you . . ."

Una broke off and her eyes narrowed as she gazed down the quiet road, only the odd passing car throwing up the dust that coated the pavement.

Maddy followed her gaze: something was on the road, something big and black that was slowly moving toward them. She stood, frozen to the spot with fascination, as every fiber in her body told her to run away screaming, watching as the object drew close and became clearer.

It was a man riding a black horse, tall and broad-shouldered, dressed from head to foot in thick, heavy black. Black leather gloves covered the huge hands that rested lightly on the reins, black leather riding boots reached above his knees. Despite the exhausting heat, his whole body was swathed in a musty black cloak. The massive animal that he rode drew level with Maddy, but she could not bring herself to look as its angry eye rolled at her. It chomped on its bit as sweat and saliva foamed and frothed down the bulging muscles in its chest. No. She looked past the animal to the tall, stiff collar of the rider's cloak, the collar standing proud around empty air, and then dropped her gaze to the rider's lap, where his head was sitting.

The pale, bald pate glowed with a sickly green light that beat against the summer haze and its small black eyes darted around in its sockets. A hideous, idiotic grin split its thin lips, and as Maddy watched the body gathered up the reins in one hand, scooped the head up with the other, and held it out to her on its massive palm.

The eyes suddenly stopped darting around and focused on Maddy's green ones, its tightly clenched teeth fell open and a black tongue caressed the air as it spoke a word, carried on a breath that smelled of sickly sweet rot.

"Maaddieee," it said.

chapter two

AS SOON AS THE LAST SYLLABLE OF HER NAME escaped those shriveled lips, the teeth snapped shut again and the monstrous faerie began to lose his grip on the mortal world. Before Maddy's eyes, he began to fade and drift apart like smoke in the wind as the binding magic of Tír na nÓg called him back. Maddy watched, transfixed, until all that was left was that rictus grin, hanging in the air like the Cheshire Cat's. As soon as it disappeared, with a pop of imploding air, she turned to look at Una.

"That was the dullahan," Maddy said, her voice shaking with fear. She felt herself choke on her words and stopped for a moment to clear her throat. "What is he doing here, so far from Liadan's court? Why did he say my name? I didn't even know he could speak!"

"He normally doesn't," said Una, her eyes fixed on the spot where the faerie had stood. "He never does, unless . . ."

"Unless what?" prompted Maddy. "Unless *what*, Una?"

The banshee gave herself a little shake and looked at Maddy, her dark eyes despairing. "He's the soul collector, Maddy. He doesn't speak except to say the name of the person whose soul he will come for next."

The world fell away under her feet as Maddy's terrified brain processed what Una had just said. The sound of her own blood roared in her ears and drowned out the noise of a car passing by and a lawnmower droning in a front yard. Her lips struggled silently to form the words that tripped and stumbled into place in her mind.

"That means . . . that means . . ." she stuttered.

"It means Liadan has put a sentence of death on you and has sent the dullahan to deliver it personally."

"So it's finally happening," said Maddy with numb lips. "She's coming after me."

"This is much, much bigger than you now," hissed Una as she pulled her rags closer around her skinny body. "You swore an oath of fealty to Meabh and the Autumn Court when you needed her protection. Remember? For Liadan to go after you, a subject of the Autumn Court, is an open declaration of war. She *cannot* attack another court like this and not expect them to retaliate."

"War?" asked Maddy.

Una nodded once, a curt bob of her head. "War," she sighed. "It has come at last. While all the Tuatha have been spoiling for it, it would *have* to be Liadan who tipped the scales. The Winter Queen is truly crazy. She will destroy everything in a fit of rage for not getting her own way."

Maddy shuddered. *What she wants is my head on a stick,* she thought. *Maybe another faerie will give it to her to avoid a war.*

Una must have been thinking the same thing. "I have to tell your granda. He can keep you safe," said Una.

"No, don't!" said Maddy.

"Why ever not, child?" asked Una, her dark eyes snapping with anger.

"We knew this was coming, Una. It's why he sent me to Cork in the first place, remember?" said Maddy. "Surround me with iron, keep the faeries away, and hope that they forget about me and we can all go back to living normal lives." She laughed, a bitter sound without humor. "I told him it wouldn't work."

"And what will keeping secrets achieve?"

"I don't want to keep secrets from him, Una, I just want time to think!" said Maddy, her voice rising with anger.

"Think about *what*?!" demanded the banshee, her own voice shrill with rage. "Do you think you can handle this on your own? Is that it? The last time you went up against the Winter Queen you nearly died—you have a lovely scar on your shoulder to remind you of that!"

"I know, but—"

"And if you're thinking Meabh is going to come to your rescue, you can think again," Una snapped.

"Meabh does nothing for anyone unless it suits her. I've seen enough of Meabh over the centuries to know that what suits her often ends in nothing but pain and trouble for others. So we are *not* going down that road!"

Maddy knew full well what Meabh thought of her. It was ten months since Maddy had pledged her allegiance to the Autumn Queen. Ten months since she had found out she was the new Hound of Ireland, thanks to the blood of heroes that ran through her veins. It didn't make much difference to Maddy's life—it gave her no superpowers, no advantages at all. The only thing it brought was trouble, as it seemed to make her irresistible to faeries and make Sighted humans—humans who, like Maddy, could see faeries—look at her as if she was an unexploded bomb. She remembered what Meabh had said to her when Maddy realized she had been tricked into swearing an oath of fealty.

Now that I've collared you and leashed you, I'll stoke those fires in you. And when the time comes and I let loose the dogs of war, the Hound of Ireland will lead my pack, baying for blood.

She swallowed. "I have no idea what I am going to do, Una, but if you give me a couple of hours I might think of something," she said.

"Oh no," said Una. "I know what kind of foolish ideas you come up with when you are left to your own devices. No, I told your granda I was going to look out for you, and that's exactly what I am going to do." Maddy watched in horror as Una's wizened little body began to ripple away from her, the little faerie moving so fast her body was a long blur that left streaks of color in the air behind, like fuel trails from a jet.

"Una, wait!" Maddy lunged at the little faerie woman but it was too late. The banshee was gone and would no doubt be talking to her granda within half an hour.

"I hate it when you do that!" shouted Maddy, even though the faerie was now long gone. The fat little man mowing his lawn gazed at her suspiciously. Maddy was suddenly very conscious that she was raving at thin air at the entrance to a home for the mentally ill. She smiled nervously at the man and then began to walk quickly in the direction of Cork city and Aunt Fionnula's house.

The dullahan was an old and powerful faerie, strong enough to pierce the barrier that kept the mortal and faerie worlds separate, even for just a few minutes. Halloween was when the barrier was weakest, the best time for the faerie to break loose, but that was still three months away. Maddy was sure there would be no other faeries stalking her as she walked home. Even so, it was an effort to stop her shaking legs from breaking into a run, to get away from green suburbia with the country-side lapping its boundaries into the iron heart of Cork city.

Maddy didn't own a summer dress, and her jeans stuck to her sweat-slicked skin, taking away all her flexibility. She felt as if she was lumbering along like a mummy and that was going to make her just as conspic-uous to a lurking faerie as it would if she sprinted home.

Sweat made her scalp itchy and her thick brown hair sat like thatch on her head, the sun beating down on it. She tried not to flinch at sudden loud noises or peer too closely at the faces of passers-by or children playing on the pavement. One little girl made her flinch, her narrow pointed face and shock of red hair as she looked up from chalking the pavement catching Maddy's eye. The flash of green eyes, the long thin bones of her hands, made Maddy suspect a faerie, but the child's eyes were clear and innocent.

Her body screamed with tension and her back was aching from the effort of keeping her muscles clenched by the time she turned on to the street where Aunt Fionnula lived. It was an ugly little road, built in the 1960s with tons of concrete to form gray houses, gray pavements, and a cracked and neglected asphalt road, but Maddy could have dropped to her knees and kissed the dusty ground. Devoid of any landscaping to soften its harshness, and with many of the tiny backyards smothered in decking, there was no lush vegetation here to attract faeries, no wood copses where trees bent feathery heads together to talk, no streams to sing to birds while their waters sparkled like diamonds in the summer sun. It was as soulless and miserable an urban environment as anyone hiding from a faerie could hope for, where every pitted, stained surface reflected the heat and the taste of dust coated Maddy's mouth. As much as Maddy hated Aunt Fionnula and hated her overcrowded, cluttered house, right now she was grateful that she lived here and not in the soft, green village of Blarney, so close to the faerie mound.

She pushed open the spindly black iron gate that marked the boundary of the house from the road. It was a tiny house, jammed tight into a terrace and, like many of their neighbors, Aunt Fionnula and Uncle Jack had concreted over the front yard so they could have off-street parking. As she walked up the path, Maddy quickly scanned the terrace to count how many other front yards were the same, how many patches of earth were crushed by slabs of concrete, seedlings choked off in the dark. The less nature she could see, the better she felt.

The front door was glazed top and bottom with a dimpled brown glass that allowed her see a watery outline of a figure standing in the hallway. From the curve of the big belly she could see it was Uncle Jack. She didn't have a front door key—she guessed her aunt didn't want her to feel like she was a member of the family or anything—so she knocked on the glass to be let in. She scanned the street behind her as she waited, her fingertips touching the smooth surface of the letter box for the comforting feel of metal. But apart from the odd car whizzing past and a few small kids playing with a skipping rope, there was not a soul to be seen.

She turned back to the door and squinted through the glass—Uncle Jack hadn't moved and it looked as if he was on the phone. Maddy hissed through her teeth with frustration and tried to ignore the sick feeling of fear in her stomach. The skin on her back crawled as she faced the door—as peaceful as things here looked, she didn't completely trust that some triple-jointed, long-nailed hand was not going to reach out and grab her. She knocked again and glared at Uncle Jack.

"Come on. What are you doing in there? What's so important you can't answer the door?" she muttered.

But still he yakked on and still he ignored her. The sweat that was trickling under her clothes now had nothing to do with the heat. A little voice in her head kept yammering at her to get inside, to get out of sight, that the longer she stood on the doorstep the more chance there was something bad was going to happen to her. Not logical, but still . . .

"Oh, screw this!" said Maddy, and leaned her thumb on the doorbell. Leaned *hard* and kept it there.

The shrill ring of the doorbell jangled through the air, and with each second that passed Maddy waited for Uncle Jack to notice she was there and walk his huge stomach the tiny distance to the front door. But he turned his broad back to the door, the phone still clamped to his ear, while a smaller, thinner figure shot like an arrow from the kitchen at the end of the hallway, a figure with an irritated walk and a dome-shaped hairstyle. Maddy's heart sank. It was Aunt Fionnula.

She yanked the door open and glared at Maddy, her penciled eyebrows shooting up her forehead, almost disappearing into her dark hair, stiff and highly flammable with its lacquer of hairspray. She had been at her part-time job today and coral-colored lipstick had wandered into the thin lines that radiated from her pinched mouth. She was squeezed into a pencil skirt and a fussy blouse, and her big feet, forced into a pair of pointed shoes, flapped on the end of her stick-thin legs like flippers. Her cold eyes scanned the street for a second, alert for gossiping neighbors, and then her bony, hard fingers clamped down on Maddy's shoulder and yanked her into the house.

"Do you HAVE to make a show of me, every chance you get?" she asked, her body quivering as she looked down at Maddy. Maddy felt a grim sense of satisfaction when she realized that, even with heels on, Aunt Fionnula did not have enough height to look down the length of her beaky nose at her. Maddy had been growing, and soon she would be as tall as her aunt.

"I just wanted to get into the house," Maddy said, her voice a low growl. Every conversation with her aunt went like this—they were like two dogs fighting over a bone. But she couldn't suppress a shudder of relief as Aunt Fionnula closed the door on the harsh sunshine. "If you gave me a key I wouldn't have to stand on the doorstep every time, banging on the door to be let in."

Aunt Fionnula narrowed her eyes at Maddy and said, "What have you done this time?"

It was only then that Maddy became aware of the unnaturally jolly tone Uncle Jack was using on the telephone as he walked away into the kitchen. A tone he normally only used with his boss or Granda. Maddy swallowed. Una must have talked to Granda already.

"Granda is on his way out here," said Aunt Fionnula.

"Right now?" asked Maddy.

Aunt Fionnula shook her head, her eyes never leaving Maddy's. "No, after dinner."

"What has that got to do with me?"

"He is insisting on coming over, for no good reason," said Aunt Fionnula. That would annoy Uncle Jack. He was always nervous around his father-in-law and he hated having him in the house.

"Why does that have anything do with me?"

Aunt Fionnula thrust her face so close to Maddy's that she could see a smear of lipstick on a yellowed front tooth as Aunt Fionnula bit her words out. "It *always* has something to do with you."

"He wants to talk to you." Uncle Jack loomed over them both, his big belly straining the buttons on his shirt. He was holding the phone out to Maddy. She took it with trembling fingers.

"Hello?"

"Una told me what happened," said Granda. His voice sounded angry and scared at the same time. "She also told me you asked her to keep it secret from me."

"Not forever," said Maddy. "Just until—"

"Just until you had time to do something stupid?"

Maddy bit her lip as Aunt Fionnula flounced off to the kitchen and Uncle Jack ambled his way to the living room opposite her, a newspaper tucked under one arm.

"I'm not stupid," she said in a low voice, tears pricking at her eyes.

Granda sighed. "I never said you were, Maddy. But you can't sort everything out on your own. People get . . . hurt, if we are not careful."

Maddy closed her eyes. Bang Bang. She thought of his grave, high up on a hill, surrounded by lush green fields. She thought of Fionn and her silvery green fingers falling into the snow.

"Granda . . ."

"Pack your things. I am moving you tonight."

"Where?"

"Somewhere you can be surrounded by iron," said Granda.

"What will Granny say if I am not living here?"

"Let me worry about that. Just get your things ready."

She heard a click and the hum of the dial tone as Granda hung up on her. She sighed and put the phone down on the glass top of the hall table. The glazed door to the living room creaked open and her cousin Danny popped his head around the frame. He looked pale and tense.

"We've got a problem," he whispered, and he jerked his head toward the TV.

Really? thought Maddy. *Let's just add it to the list.*

But she said nothing and simply slipped into the room, where she perched awkwardly on the arm of the sofa. It was a long and narrow room, lined with an overstuffed sofa and equally corpulent armchairs, all shoved tight against the walls in a vain attempt to create an illusion of space. It might have worked, had

Aunt Fionnula not been so fond of patterns. They were everywhere, from the swirling carpet to the floral sofa to the stripes and borders and polka dots on the wall. The only plain things in the room were the burgundy-colored velvet curtains that hung in dusty swags from the small window. A mahogany-veneer display cabinet groaned with china figurines and framed photos. When it was switched off, the television was the simplest thing in the room and ironically the most peaceful place for Maddy to rest her eyes. The flat screen was too narrow for Aunt Fionnula to balance ornaments or dried flower displays on.

The local news was playing and Maddy came in just in time to see a familiar face flash up onscreen. She felt the blood drain from her cheeks and flicked a quick glance at Uncle Jack to see if he had noticed her reaction, but he had his newspaper held firmly in front of his face so he could ignore his son and inconvenient niece and read undisturbed. Dimly, Maddy became aware of what the newscaster was saying.

"Canine experts from Fota Wildlife Park have been called in to help the local Gardaí search for what some witnesses have claimed is a wolf running loose in the grounds of Blarney Castle," said some bland-looking man in a suit that didn't fit properly. "A spokesperson for the Gardaí has said there are no animals missing from the wildlife park or from local zoos and that it is likely a large domestic dog, but that people should avoid approaching the animal and call the Gardaí if they see it."

As the newscaster talked, an image flashed up on the screen. It was a fuzzy picture taken on a cell phone by someone with a shaky hand. But there was no mistaking that silvery fur or the way the tongue lolled through those wide, open jaws. Or how those black lips turned up ever so slightly, making the animal look as if it were laughing.

It was Nero.

chapter three

DANNY STOOD UP QUICKLY, HIS FACE AS WHITE as paper, as the newscaster moved on to another story. He plucked quickly at the short sleeve of Maddy's T-shirt and nodded his head toward the stairs. She flicked another glance at Uncle Jack, who was still trying to pretend he was alone in the room, and followed Danny out. Aunt Fionnula was banging pots and pans in the kitchen, cooking dinner in her own vengeful way. And the house only got noisier as they climbed the stairs.

Even without Aunt Fionnula's tragic love of pattern and ornament, the house would have felt claustrophobic with all the people living in it. Maddy had a sneaking suspicion Aunt Fionnula didn't really like children, yet she had managed to have five of her own. The entire family was squeezed into a three-bedroom terrace house. Life had been a little easier since an extension had been built as a bedroom for Aunt Fionnula and Uncle Jack and they could give the upstairs of their house to their children. But the little house still shook to the sound of boisterous boys—the thudding of their feet, their squeals as games got rough, the blare of music and video games and clatter and crunch as their debris was kicked and stood on.

As the only girl in the family, Maddy's cousin Roisin had the privilege of a room all to herself, even if it was a tiny box room. It was the calmest, quietest, and most private place in the house and Danny headed straight there as his brothers did their best to kill each other in the largest bedroom, kicking and rolling on fallen toys and clothes. Maddy faltered and watched them for a second. Sean was kicking Ronan in the ribs and screaming, "Take it back, TAKE IT BACK!" He was so red in the face he looked as if he might explode. Paul was squealing with delight and jumping up and down on the top bunk bed as he egged his brother on, eyes sparkling. Maddy winced at the thudding noise Sean's sneaker-clad feet made as they hit Ronan's ribs.

It was a mistake to stop. It distracted the horrors. They jumped up and ran to the door to see what Maddy and Danny were up to.

"Ooooh, you're going into a *girl's* room," crowed Ronan, while Sean and Paul erupted into laughter. "Are you going to play with their dollies? Are you going to put on lipstick?" Sean puckered up and made kissing noises while fluttering his eyelashes.

"You won't be so funny if I come over there and give you a pasting," said Danny, trying to fix them with his most threatening glare.

"Go ahead, try it, I dare ya!" said Paul. "You know I can burst ya!"

"It'll be worth it," said Danny.

The two boys glared at each other and flexed imaginary muscles. Maddy rolled her eyes. It really was survival of the fittest in this house.

"Why are you going into Ro's room anyway?" asked Ronan, who had always been the slightly smarter one. "We're not allowed in there."

"None of your business," said Danny.

"If you're going into Ro's room, then so are we!" said Sean, whom Maddy had always considered the slightly thicker one.

Danny opened his mouth to argue with them just as they decided to charge. Maddy shoved him through the half-open door and they managed to slam it shut as the three boys collided with it. Danny kept the door handle up as one of them tried to force it down from the other side, while the other two, probably Sean and Paul, beat on the wood with their fists and feet, howling to be let in. The metal of the handle began to bite into Danny's hand as it slowly moved down—Ronan must have been hanging off it on the other side, using all his body weight to try to force it down. Maddy put her palms flat against the door and leaned against it to give Danny a hand when she heard Uncle Jack shout, "If you break another door in this house, you won't see daylight for a month!"

The three monsters gave a shriek and ran back to the big bedroom. Maddy heard their door slam and their muffled giggles and snorts. She turned and leaned her back against the door and gave a sigh of relief. Roisin was sitting on her bed, a book on her lap. She sighed and shook her head.

"I can't wait until I can move out and get a bit of peace."

The box room would have been small with just Roisin's single bed and her chest of drawers squeezed into it, the armoir hulking by the window and blocking some of the light, but with a mattress laid on the floor for Maddy to sleep on and her stuff spilling out of three knapsacks, there literally wasn't room to stand. To get to their clothes, the girls had to walk on Maddy's bed. Maddy and Roisin were good friends, even now, but Maddy missed her own room at Granny and Granda's, even if it did have wedding-paper wallpaper.

Danny flung himself on the mattress while Maddy sank down next to Roisin.

"So you've seen the news then?" asked Roisin.

Maddy nodded. "Is it definitely Nero?"

"If it's not, it's doing a very good impression of him," said Danny.

"There have been a few pictures taken, not just the one shown on the TV," said Roisin. "They're all over the Internet. People are posting comments on Face-book and Twitter from experts saying it's a wolf."

Maddy snorted. "Everyone's an expert online."

"Yes," said Roisin. "But it's Nero. Things must be bad if he's here."

The wolves of Tír na nÓg were frightened of the mortal world, having been hunted almost to extinction when they last lived in it. Only pure desperation would drive one of them across the border between Tír na nÓg and the mortal world.

"Well, things are about to get worse," said Maddy. She took a deep breath. "The dullahan breached the border and appeared to me outside Great-Aunt Kitty's home. He said my name."

Danny and Roisin looked at each other, puzzled. "So?" said Danny.

"So Una told me that the dullahan is the soul collec-tor. He only speaks your name when yours is the next soul he's coming for."

Danny's jaw dropped and Roisin went white, mak-ing her ginger freckles stand out. "You're dying?" she asked.

"No, I'm perfectly healthy," said Maddy. "It means that someone wants me dead."

"Liadan," said Danny and Roisin at the same time. Maddy nodded miserably.

"But she can't do that!" said Roisin. "You're a subject of the Autumn Court. She can't attack someone else's subject without . . . without . . ."

". . . declaring war on the court." Danny said the words his sister could not.

They all looked at each other in silence. War. They had faced the abyss once before, had clung to its edge and peered into its darkness, but both worlds had been pulled back from the brink just in time. But Liadan's move had sent Maddy tumbling into its maw, and as she fell she dragged the Winter and Autumn Courts with her. No doubt the Spring and Summer Courts would rush to join the bloodshed, their monarchs eager for a fight. She had no idea whose side they would be on.

"We knew this was going to happen," said Roisin. Maddy looked at her, but Roisin shrugged. "Well, we did. You said it yourself, Maddy—they were never going to give up, never going to stop coming after you. Liadan has wanted you dead for ages and Meabh is just fascinated with you being the Hound. She thinks it's going to tip a war in her favor, having you tied to the court. God only knows why."

Last Halloween Maddy had found out that she was the new Hound of Ireland, destined to follow in the footsteps of Cú Chulainn, an ancient Irish hero, the only mortal Maddy knew of who had taken on the faeries and won. It was up to Maddy now to be as strong as him, and to keep the mortal world safe. She had no idea how she was supposed to do that, and Meabh had laughed at her for even thinking she could try, but the Autumn Queen had been very keen to put a collar around Maddy's neck and bring her into her court.

"Anyone sort of relieved this has happened?" asked Danny.

"Are you insane?" said Maddy.

"Sometimes I think I am," said Danny. "I don't sleep too well at night; I have screaming nightmares when I do. I jump at every shadow and I can't tell anyone else about any of this, and even if I could, who would believe me?"

"Cassandra syndrome," said Roisin.

"What?" said Danny.

"It's what everyone's got in that home, including Aunt Kitty," said Roisin. "They know what's going on, but when they tell people, no one believes them and either they get locked up for being mentally ill or the fear of what's coming drives them crazy anyway."

"Who's Cassandra?" asked Maddy.

"She was the daughter of King Priam of Troy," said Roisin. "She was cursed to have the gift of prophecy but never to be believed. She knew Troy was going to burn, she saw all those people dying in her dreams long before it happened, but no one listened."

"Yeah, that sounds about right," Danny muttered.

They sat in silence for a while, lost in their own thoughts, when Roisin said, "I want this to be over."

She carried on talking while Maddy and Danny stared at her.

"I'm getting the screaming nightmares too, and so are you, Maddy. We share a room; it's pointless trying to hide it. But the nightmares don't go away, even when I'm awake. I keep seeing them, beneath the mound, under my feet, staring up with those pale faces, just waiting to break through and kill everyone around them while they set themselves up as kings and queens again."

"I'm not sure that they are technically under our feet . . ." said Maddy.

"I don't care about the physics of it!" said Roisin. "They're there and they want to kill us all, or at least enough of us so we never think about fighting back again, ever, and I can't just forget that. I can't go to school and live my life and put it to one side that they are constantly probing the barrier, trying to find a way through, that a war in Ireland, if not another world war, is possible. And the Sighted are the only ones who know about it and the only ones who can see it coming."

She sighed and rubbed her forehead with her fingertips. "I just want to be able to sleep again, you know? Have a proper sleep. You keep saying you just want life to go back to normal, Maddy, but it won't. I'm tired of waiting for them to come get us. We have to finish this."

"How are we supposed to do that?" asked Maddy.

"I don't know," said Roisin. "But it starts with you, so it has to finish with you."

"You're the one who draws them, Maddy," said Danny. "Even Granda said he had never seen so many faeries about the place until you came."

Maddy looked at her cousins. It was true—their faces were pale and tired and marked by worry. She probably didn't look much better herself. Danny's clothes hung from his frame and it wasn't just because he was growing so fast. Roisin, who had always been teased for being fat, was also looking a lot more slender. Her broad cheekbones were standing out in sharp relief below her shadow-smudged eyes. Her eyes were huge in her face, twin pools of melting chocolate, while her red curls fizzed against her pallid skin. Maddy had thought her cousin's face had simply been changing as she grew up—now she realized Roisin was stressed almost beyond endurance. She had been so wrapped up in her own misery she hadn't noticed that her cousins, just like her, were still carrying around the events of last year in their minds, playing them out in their dreams, their tongues locked inside their mouths.

"You know we could die?" she asked.

"Meh." Danny shrugged. "What's new?"

"At least I'd sleep," said Roisin. She smiled, as if it was supposed to be funny. But they all knew it wasn't.

"So where do we start?" asked Danny.

"We have to get to Blarney and find Nero," said Maddy. "He loses all power of speech this side of the barrier, but we have to get him back to Tír na nÓg. He must be looking for us."

Roisin nodded in agreement. "We have to get all four of us back through the mound, and then we can find out what is going on, what drove him here."

"And then we'll have a good reason to pick a fight," said Danny.

Then the other bit of bad news dawned on Maddy. "Granda is on his way here, straight after dinner."

"Why?" said Danny.

"Una told him about the dullahan, so now he's talking about moving me somewhere safer," said Maddy, while Roisin groaned and Danny swore.

"That's it then, isn't it? We're finished!" said Roisin, punching her legs with frustration. "We can't just head out for Blarney now. Mom will never let us out of the house and Granda will be here before we can sneak away and then you'll be gone. Myself and Danny can't do this without you!"

"I know," said Maddy. "I don't know what to do."

"We need to stop him getting here, buy enough time so that we can sneak out tonight when everyone is asleep. Mom and Dad know nothing about Tír na nÓg or what's been going on; they won't be watching us in case we sneak out in the middle of the night. But Granda will—we've tried that trick too often. Once he's here, there'll be no getting away from him."

"How are we supposed to do that?" asked Maddy.

"Meabh," said Danny.

Roisin's head snapped back up and hope bloomed again in her eyes. "Yes, of course, why didn't I think of that?!" she said. "She's bound to help—she wants you back in Tír na nÓg, especially if there is going to be a fight."

"How am I supposed to ask her?"

"Talk to the air," said Roisin. "She's always listening, isn't she?"

"But what can she do?" asked Maddy. "It's summer. I don't know how powerful she can be out of her season."

"She's a monarch and a witch," said Danny. "She's pretty strong."

"This alliance of yours has gotten us into enough trouble," said Roisin. "We might as well get something out of it for once."

Maddy took a deep breath. "Fine," she said. "I'll do it right after . . ."

"Dinner!" shrieked Aunt Fionnula from the bottom of the stairs.

chapter four

THE CALL FOR FOOD WAS ENOUGH TO SEND THE monsters into a frenzy. They yanked their bedroom door back so hard the g-force nearly sucked Maddy into the room. She stood back and let them charge on ahead of her, whooping. Roisin rolled her eyes. "You'd swear they were never fed."

The kitchen was unbearably hot and steamy. Aunt Fionnula was opening a window for a bit of relief as Maddy walked in. She noticed that although the room was as steamy as a sauna, it didn't wilt her aunt's helmet of hair, not even a tiny bit. Aunt Fionnula snapped orders at Sean, Ronan, and Paul as they crowded around her while she tried to serve up the sausages, mash, and beans.

"DON'T touch the pot, it's hot; keep your hands out of the beans, you haven't even washed them, Sean. PUT THAT BREAD BACK, you do not need bread with your dinner!"

She nodded her head absentmindedly while Roisin, Danny, and the monsters talked to her. She slid Maddy's dinner over to her without so much as a look and Maddy silently picked up her fork and began to eat. She noticed Aunt Fionnula was preparing a tray for herself and Uncle Jack, which meant they were having a TV dinner.

"Eat everything up now and rinse off your plates in the sink, I'm not chiseling mash off all night," she said, before letting the kitchen door swing shut behind her as she tottered off down the hallway to the living room with the tray loaded with food and cutlery.

The monsters went deadly quiet, watching her retreating back with sparkling eyes, cocking their heads for the sound of the living room door shutting and the volume on the TV rising. And then the entertainment started.

Ronan was first with a massive belch.

"Stop it, that's disgusting!" said Roisin, while Danny tried to hide a smile behind his hand. The monsters howled with laughter and began to belch together like a demented bullfrog chorus.

"Stop it right now or I am telling Mom!" said Roisin, her voice rising.

"Look, Ro!" said Sean, opening his mouth and sticking out a tongue loaded with chewed-up food.

"Sean, what has Mom said . . ." Ro paused. "WHAT is that smell? Oh, Paul, you haven't."

"I haven't!" he said, shoving a sausage into his mouth.

"You have!" asked Roisin. "That's horrible. We're eating!"

"The one who smelt it dealt it," sang Sean.

"The one who said the rhyme did the crime," said Danny, which had the monsters roaring with laughter again, food and spit spraying across the table.

Roisin threw her fork down in disgust. "Honestly, it's like trying to eat with chimpanzees."

While the monsters baited Roisin, Maddy looked at the glass in the kitchen door. The door to the living room stayed firmly closed and there was no sign of Aunt Fionnula or Uncle Jack coming to break up the party. Clearly her aunt and uncle were tired after working all day and in no mood to do any crowd control. It was now or never.

She put her fork down. "I'm going outside. The smell in here is awful," she announced, getting up from her seat. She couldn't help but flick a glance at Roisin and Danny, who both looked at her and away again quickly. It was too obvious and the monsters picked up on it.

"Why are you going outside?" asked Ronan, his eyes narrowed with suspicion. "What's so great about outside?"

"None of your business," said Maddy.

"I'm telling Mammy you didn't eat your dinner," said Paul.

"Like I care," said Maddy, heading for the back door.

"I'm coming too," said Ronan, getting up from his seat and launching himself at the door. Maddy lunged ahead of him and managed to get through the door before he did, but she wasn't quick enough to shut it on him. He jammed his body between the door and the kitchen wall, his fingers wrapped around the door frame and his arm up to stop Maddy from closing it on him.

"C'mere to me, you," said Danny as he walked up behind Ronan and grabbed him under the arms, wrenching him away from the door. Ronan gave a howl of rage and swung around, throwing a wild punch that missed Danny by a mile. "Let me go, or I'll burst ya!"

"Push me and I'll beat you good-looking," Maddy heard Danny say as he slammed the door shut. "And it would take me hours!"

Maddy sighed with relief as Danny blocked the doorway and the double glazing muffled the howls of rage from both boys. She walked across the tiny garden, its grass worn away by the monsters, littered with soccer balls, a mini-trampoline, and a broken set of goalposts, and headed for the biggest piece of greenery around.

The house behind had a mature oak tree at the end of their backyard that spread its branches over Aunt Fionnula's fence. Uncle Jack was constantly grumbling about it and telling the neighbors to cut it down, claiming it cast too much shade over his yard.

Maddy turned her face up to the tree, hearing its broad leaves rattle as a summer breeze stroked their tips. She closed her eyes and listened to the sounds of life all around her. Somewhere a dog was barking, a dull monotonous sound devoid of all passion. Children were playing in their yards and some of the neighbors were indulging in the great Irish summer tradition of burned barbecue. Danny and the monsters were still rioting in the kitchen behind her.

Maddy knew if Meabh was listening, a whisper would be loud enough for her voice to reach the witch queen's ears. When Maddy had given the Queen of Autumn her oath of fealty last year, she had choked it out as she was being dangled in the air by Fachtna, another homicidal Winter faerie. Meabh had heard all right, and as she had promised, she came straight to Maddy's aid. But the barrier between the two worlds had been failing then and the faeries had been finding it easy to slip between the worlds. Plus, it had been autumn, when Meabh was strongest. Now the barrier was strong again and it was summer, Queen Niamh's season to rule. Maddy didn't know if Meabh would be able to hear her, much less do anything to help her.

She looked up at the oak tree, such a strong and majestic reminder of nature, here, in the middle of the city. Its whispering leaves spoke of green fields and tall grasses, deer stepping carefully through woodland and floating clouds.

"My queen," she said, talking directly to the tree, "help me. You wanted this fight and you wanted me in it. I can't escape this house without help, and once Granda is here I won't be going anywhere. If you want the Hound to run for you, then you need to make it happen. I can't get to Tír na nÓg on my own."

The branches above her head dipped and the leaves rustled just a little more loudly.

Ask me nicely, they whispered, and for a moment Maddy smelled rain. Startled, she searched the tree's foliage, looking for a flash of red hair, a gleam of gold jewelry, or the sight of a bright-green eye staring back at her from the fluttering leaves. Nothing.

She searched her mind for suitable phrases she had read in fantasy novels and took a deep breath.

"I beseech you, my queen, aid your humble subject in her hour of need," said Maddy, trying and not really succeeding in keeping the sting of sarcasm from her voice. The sound of thunder grumbled in the distance, shocking everyone around her into momentary silence. Even the dog paused in its barking. Maddy shifted nervously from foot to foot. Perhaps she should have tried to sound a bit more sincere?

Better, the leaves whispered. *But I could have done without your tone.*

"Sorry," Maddy muttered.

The tree said nothing more. Dark clouds began to build up, piling on each other as they rushed to obscure the sun. The temperature dropped a couple of degrees as the sunny backyard was thrown into shade and a chilly wind began to blow around Maddy's ears. She let out a long sigh of relief and let her body relax. Maddy had no idea what Meabh was up to, but it was obvious she had heard her and had the power to act. All she could do now was sit tight and see what happened.

She had just turned to walk back into the house when a flicker of movement caught her eye. It was Una, crouched in the corner of the yard, her rags wrapped tightly around her withered body. She was rocking backward and forward, tears streaking silently down her wrinkled cheeks while her soft eyes locked onto Maddy.

"So you're back, are you?" asked Maddy. "I'm a bit angry at you for tattling on me to Granda."

"I had to," said Una, "for your own good."

"When people do things to me I don't like," said Maddy, "it doesn't make me feel any better."

"You have no idea what you have done," said Una.

Maddy shrugged. "Probably not. But I had to do s*omething*."

Una shook her head, her face gleaming silver with the tracks of her tears. "Foolish child. Arrogant Hound."

Maddy sighed. "You're always trying, but I'm still here and the world hasn't ended yet. I'm still alive, aren't I?"

"No," said Una. "You're just not dead yet."

"There's no talking to you when you're in this mood," said Maddy. "I'm going to finish my dinner and get some sleep. Stick around if you plan on being helpful."

The little banshee just sniffed and looked away, an expression of disgust on her face.

"Suit yourself," said Maddy, as she walked back into the house.

chapter five

WITHIN TWO HOURS THE WIND WAS A RAGING
beast, howling and battering its way up and down the
street. It shook windows, knocked over trashcans, and
screamed through cracks around doors. The clouds
piled up one on top of the other in soft charcoal folds
and then unleashed the rain from their bellies. It hammered from the sky and bounced on the dusty pavement like stones. Soon the gutter was transformed into a
muddy flood, litter and leaves swirled out of sight while
water ran down the road in rippling sheets. Sodden bar-
becues were abandoned, children were yanked indoors
no matter how badly they wanted to go out in their rubber boots and splash in the rain, and that annoying
dog was silenced. It got so dark everyone switched on
the lights in their houses, although no one pulled their

curtains. As far as Maddy could see, most of the neighbors were standing in front of their windows, gazing open-mouthed at the shrieking storm that had blown up out of nowhere in the middle of one of the hottest summers Ireland had ever known. Even the monsters were stunned into silence, their grubby fingers clinging to the windowsill as they gazed at the chaotic sky.

The TV continued to flicker away in its corner as news bulletins warned of falling trees and flooded roads. "Freak weather conditions have been caused by an unforeseen collision of warm and cold air fronts over the Irish Sea," said a rather frazzled-looking weather forecaster. "The storm is expected to die out in the early hours of the morning, but until then the public are advised not to make any unnecessary journeys."

Maddy felt her heart lift a little bit when she heard this. Did this mean Granda would be trapped in Blarney tonight? Or would he send another Sighted to come get her? But it would have to be someone Aunt Fionnula knew. Even she wouldn't hand Maddy over to a complete stranger.

"It's freezing," complained Danny. "Can't we stick the fire on?"

"Do I look as if I am made of money?!" barked Uncle Jack, as the phone started to ring in the hallway. "I'm not putting the heating on in July. If you're cold, put a sweater on."

Aunt Fionnula walked into the room and held the phone out to Maddy. "It's Granda, for you."

Maddy cautiously pressed the phone to her ear. "Hello?"

"I can't get out there until the storm is over," said Granda, and she could hear him grinding his teeth in frustration. "Awful handy this storm, isn't it?"

Maddy felt her bowels turn to water. How much did Granda know? Had Una told him she was sworn to the Autumn Court? Granda was terrified of the Tuatha de Dannan, Meabh most of all—he'd hit the roof if he knew. While her mind worked at a million miles an hour, Granda sighed.

"I will be there first thing," he said. "Don't do anything stupid, Maddy. Just go to bed tonight and wait for me to come get you in the morning. I mean that. No sneaking out in the middle of the night."

"No, Granda." The lie tripped so easily from her tongue. But she didn't really think he believed her— sneaking out in the middle of the night was what she did. He was hardly expecting her to change now, was he?

"Be a good girl, Maddy," said Granda. "One day you will have children of your own, and then you will know what an awful thing it is to worry about them. Let me talk to your cousins now."

I'd be a good girl, thought Maddy as she handed the phone to Roisin, *if it ever got me anywhere.*

⤳

Tucked up in bed that night she listened to the rain thundering against the window. Despite the drop in temperature, the room still felt stuffy with every window in the house sealed tight against the water. She was wearing jeans, a T-shirt, and a hoodie. The duvet was pulled up under her chin in case Aunt Fionnula decided to check on them before she went to bed. But everyone in the house had settled for the night and the bedroom door had not creaked open once.

She rolled onto her side and thought about the force of the storm. It was terrifying what Meabh could do even when she wasn't the Tuatha in power, even in the mortal world. She thought about what the news presenter had said, about a warm and a cold front colliding, and imagined a blond queen and a red-haired one fighting above the Irish Sea.

"Are you still awake, Ro?" she whispered in the dark.

"Course I am," said Roisin, her voice muffled by her duvet. "I can't sleep when I'm petrified."

"You don't have to come with me, you know," said Maddy. "I'm not going to think you're a coward or anything."

"I *am* a coward," whispered Roisin. "But staying here, wondering what is going on when everyone else is carrying on with life the same as usual, is going to make me nuts. And we've all seen where you go when *that* happens."

Maddy thought about this for a second. "Horrible, isn't it, being Sighted?"

"Yes," sighed Roisin, and then she was quiet again.

Maddy listened to Roisin's quiet breathing, the soft rustle of her clothes. She wondered if her cousin had managed to fall asleep after all. Outside the rain stopped roaring down and began a gentler, softer whisper against the glass panes. Maddy had no idea how much time had gone by when the door to the room opened a few inches and Danny slipped his body sideways through the small gap, trying to avoid the point where the hinges would creak loudly in the silence of the sleeping house.

"Time to go," he whispered, handing Maddy and Roisin a small knapsack each as they kicked back their duvets and began to pull their sneakers on. Maddy looked at her watch. Four a.m. She rubbed at her eyes.

"What's in the bags?" asked Roisin.

"A change of clothes, some bars of chocolate, a flashlight each."

"Blimey, you're organized," whispered Maddy.

Danny shrugged. "I had a feeling we were going to have to go back in. So I stowed these away under my bed, just in case."

"Good thinking," said Roisin.

"Any proper food in here?" asked Maddy.

"Oh, come on!" said Danny. "I've had these under my bed for months—fresh food would have evolved by now. I wouldn't have had to pack it; it would have been able to walk after us."

"We can always stop at the gas station and get some sandwiches," said Roisin.

"Weapons?" asked Maddy.

Danny shook his head. "We don't have any iron in the house that can be used as a weapon, sorry. We've all got iron on us. It will have to do."

Maddy clambered over her own bed and eased the armoir door open, bracing it with her palm so the pressure catch would not open too fast and too hard and make a loud click. She grabbed her fake leather jacket and felt for the lump in the lining where she had hidden a crude iron knife that Granda had made for her. She was going to roast, wearing the jacket in this heat. She could already feel the temperature begin to climb as the storm blew itself out. And she had no more knives for Danny and Roisin. It was meager protection, but she felt it was better than nothing.

She took a deep breath and shrugged the jacket on before looking at her cousins' white faces floating in the dark, their pale skin picked out by wan rays of moonlight.

"Let's go," she said.

Ronan was fast asleep in the room he shared with Danny, starfished in his boxer shorts on top of a rumpled duvet. The door to the bedroom where Sean and Paul slept was slightly ajar and they were unconscious from a day of kicking, gouging, and biting. Danny jerked his head toward the stairs and they crept down them as quietly as they could, wincing at every creak the steps made beneath the floral carpet. Aunt Fionnula and Uncle Jack were fast asleep at the back of the house and Danny took great care not to rattle the keys on the hook beside the door as he lifted them off. He turned the keys slowly in the locks, so the tumblers turned with sleepy clicks, and one by one they tiptoed out into the moonlit, drizzly summer night.

Although the temptation to run was overwhelming, they walked gingerly on their cushioned feet down the dark terrace and Maddy didn't dare breathe normally until they had reached the top of the ancient steps that led them down the hill and into the heart of the city. She gripped the narrow railing that ran up the middle and watched her feet carefully on the wet, shining stone.

"How are we going to get to Blarney?" asked Roisin as they hurried down the long flight of steps. "It's miles away."

"We're going to get a cab," said Danny. "But we have to start walking toward the village. I'm not going into a taxi office—they'll call the guards on us. We have to make someone feel sorry for us."

"But we haven't got any money," said Maddy.

"We do," said Danny.

"How?" asked Rosin.

"I stole the monsters' birthday money out of Mom's chest of drawers," said Danny.

"Oh God," said Roisin. "We're never going to be able to go home—Mom is going to skin us alive when she finds out!"

"I can't worry about that right now," said Danny. "Let's just get to Blarney."

It would be a nice problem to have, thought Maddy. *If we're worrying about Aunt Fionnula finding out the birthday money is gone, it means we came back.* She knew Roisin and Danny were thinking the same thing, but they all avoided looking at each other. At the bottom of the steps, Danny turned away from the quays at the heart of the city and instead followed the road that joined up with the freeway, the road that would lead them away from the safety of the iron-clad city and into the fields and woods of the countryside, the road that would eventually lead to the faerie mound that pulsed like a tumor in the grounds of Blarney Castle.

chapter six

THE FREEWAY WAS LIT UP ALMOST AS BRIGHT AS day with giant arching sodium lights and clusters of road signs, each group with its own white light to combat the sulfur. Despite the lateness of the hour, the road leading to it was still quite busy. No one seemed to notice the three children walking along, although one truck driver did sound his horn in a blaring blast that made Maddy jump out of her skin, but he didn't stop. She was wide awake and jittery with lack of sleep. The lights hurt her eyes and she felt a bit nauseated.

They walked for a little while, cringing at every car that passed them in case the driver stopped and tried to make them go home, while looking over their shoulders to see if it was a taxi. When they drew level with the Blackrock Shopping Center, Roisin refused to walk any farther.

"We're going to be walking on the freeway at this rate and it's not safe," she said, when Danny tried to persuade her.

"We have to keep walking," Danny said.

"Why?" asked Roisin. "We're supposed to be getting a lift anyway. There's no point in hiding from all the traffic, is there, or scurrying away from everyone?"

"We might have to," said Maddy glumly. "There is no way a taxi driver is going to take us out to Blarney at four thirty in the morning."

"What *are* we going to say if a taxi does come along?" asked Roisin.

"Leave that to me," said Danny. "I'll think of something."

So Roisin and Maddy slumped to the ground and sat cross-legged with bowed heads, fighting their tiredness and closing their eyes against the glare of the lights. Maddy's eyes ached and the car headlights were painful as they swept over her face. Danny stood by the side of the road watching the traffic coming out of Cork and chewing on a cuticle.

Despite the tension, Maddy found herself dozing off. Her head nodded against her chest and snapped forward, waking her up with a jerk. Her eyelids flicked open and she gazed at the deserted shopping center, still lit up with lights trained on storefronts and signs even though there was no one awake to go shopping. She found herself thinking of her lumpy double bed in

Granny and Granda's spare room with its fussy, shiny wallpaper. She wished she was tucked up in it right now, thinking the thoughts she used to think when the biggest problems in her life were hating Blarney and missing her parents. The good old days.

"Taxi!" yelped Danny, frantically waving his arm up and down as a taxi put on its indicator and pulled up a few feet away from them. Danny grabbed his knapsack and yanked a sleepy Roisin to her feet. "Just hop right in," he said. "He'll find it harder to get rid of us."

Danny jogged along the pavement, opened the rear passenger door and dived on to the backseat, Roisin and Maddy piling in right behind him.

"Whoa, whoa, whoa, hold your horses!" said the driver, twisting around in his seat to glare at them. "I never said I was taking you all anywhere—what are you doing out and about at this time of night anyway?"

"We need to get to Blarney, our granda is really sick," said Danny.

The taxi driver, a dark-haired man with red, tired eyes and stubble shadowing his jaw, snorted. "A likely story. Why aren't your parents driving you out there, eh?"

"They went out to him before the storm started and then they must have had to stay there. We haven't heard from them and we can't stay in the house all night on our own."

"Give me their number and I'll call them," said the man.

Danny shook his head. "You can't. My mom left her phone at home and my da isn't picking his up—the battery has probably died on him. No one is picking up the landline either—my granda's phone must have been cut off by the storm."

"They're probably on their way back out to you," said the driver. "Imagine what they'll think when they come home and find you three gone."

"They'd have been home by now," said Danny. "Something is really wrong. We need to get out to them and there's no one at home who can take us."

The taxi driver said nothing but kept glaring at them, his eyes lingering on Maddy a little bit longer than she thought necessary.

"Please help us—our granda could be dying," pleaded Roisin.

"We've got money, if that's what you're worried about. You'll get your fare," said Danny, digging into his jeans pocket.

"I don't want your money," snapped the taxi driver. "It's not getting paid I'm worrying about, it's getting charged with kidnapping." All three of them stared back at him while he looked at Maddy, the car pinging gently as it reminded him there were three people in it with no seat belts on and the engine was running.

"Who did you say your granda was?" he asked Maddy.

"We didn't. He's Bartholomew Kiely," said Danny, trying to attract his attention away from Maddy.

The taxi driver looked back at Danny and thought again for a moment. "I'll tell you what I'll do," he said. "I'll take you to the door of the house, but I'm getting out of the car with you and I want to talk to an adult, do you hear me? Otherwise, it's back in the car for the bunch of you and off to the nearest Garda station, where I'll be leaving you. Do you understand?"

"Yes," they all said at once, grabbing at the seat belts and buckling up.

"And you can put your money away, boy—I'm off the clock," said the driver. "I was heading home anyway."

"Thank you," said Danny.

Roisin looked at Maddy and gave her a little smile as the car pulled away from the curb and began to pick up speed. Maddy knew what she was thinking. They would be able to give the monsters their birthday money back. One less thing to get into trouble over.

The driver seemed to have bought their story, but Maddy was still stiff with tension. It was stuffy in the car and her jacket was too hot and heavy. She could feel her T-shirt begin to cling to her back, and her knapsack was digging into her spine. To make things worse, the driver had one of those horrible car fresheners swinging from his rearview mirror and the sickly scent of fake pine was making her stomach churn. She pressed the button in the door of the car and let the window slide down a few inches, enough for her to gulp at the balmy summer air and settle her stomach a little.

The smooth surface of the freeway hummed beneath the wheels of the car and the engine purred along. She looked at her watch—it would only take about fifteen minutes to get to Blarney at this rate. She looked at the driver and caught him looking at her in the mirror. He looked away again quickly, but not fast enough for her not to see the anger and the fear in his eyes.

Her breath froze in her throat. She thought of what the Blarney Stone had said to her when it had declared her the new Hound. *"Men may sing of your deeds when you are long dead, but they will curse you while you live!"*

He didn't ask us for the address! He knows who Granda is, he knows who I am, where we live. He's Sighted!

She looked at Roisin and Danny beside her. Roisin was rubbing her fingertips around her eyes and stretching the lids in an effort to keep alert. Danny was back chewing on his fingernails and staring out of the window. Neither of them seemed to notice anything was wrong. Perhaps the driver had given them enough of an argument to fool them into thinking getting the lift had been harder than it really was.

Anyone else would have brought us straight to the Guards, thought Maddy. *He's making sure I don't get away and bring trouble into Blarney.*

She swallowed and looked out the window again. The streetlights rushed past at frightening speed—she needed time to think. Tentatively she tried the door handle while keeping her eyes trained on the driver, but it was child-locked. She watched the road speed by beneath the car's wheels and chewed on her lower lip. She had to get out of this car.

It began to turn in a smooth bend as they followed the road to Blarney. There was the castle, a black mono- lith against the indigo sky, featureless in the night and hulking. At its feet was the mound. It couldn't be more than three quarters of a mile away.

She gripped the door handle until her knuckles turned white. "I'm going to be sick," she said. Roisin practically scrambled into Danny's lap to get away from her. "Please, stop the car. I'm going to be sick!"

"You're joking?" said the driver, but he put his foot on the brake and began to slow the car down.

Maddy clamped her hand over her mouth and heaved, making retching noises.

"Oh for the love of God, hold it in, I just had the car cleaned!" snapped the driver as he pulled in to the side of the road. The door handle sprang open and Maddy leaped from the car, raced to a wooden post-and-rail fence, and vaulted over it.

She could hear shouts from behind her as she dashed into tall grass and trees, praying she wouldn't turn her ankle on the rough ground. She stumbled and almost fell as she ran blindly into a hollow, then she tucked and rolled, pushing her face against the ground and her hands inside her jacket to stop the moonlight from pick- ing out her pale skin. She could hear the driver crashing through the undergrowth, his grunts of effort and his curses as he searched for her in the dark. She kept her body still and her breathing shallow as she heard him stop just a few feet away from her.

"You might as well make this easy on yourself," he called. "In five minutes the Sighted are going to be looking for you, and your granda won't be able to protect you this time. Come out now and I'll take you straight to him." He waited for a few seconds and then began to walk away in the direction of the castle. Maddy started to relax until she heard the sound of a number being dialed on a cell phone.

She waited until the sounds of the man's footsteps disappeared before cautiously getting to her feet and slowly making her way back to the car, careful to make as little noise as possible.

Danny and Roisin were still sitting in the back-seat. Their mouths opened as Maddy appeared in the headlights. The engine was still running so she walked around to the driver's seat, turned the engine off, and flung the keys into the nearest bushes.

"What are you doing?" asked Danny.

"He knows who we are," said Maddy. "Anyone else notice he didn't need an address in Blarney? He knew just where to take us."

"Oh," said Roisin as the realization dawned on her.

"And now he's calling the Sighted to let them know we're here," Maddy went on. "So if we want to have a hope of making it to the mound before they do, we'd better start running."

"What about Nero?" asked Roisin as she and Danny scrambled out of the car with their bags. "We can't just leave him!"

"We have no choice, Ro," said Maddy. "If we stop to look for Nero, we'll never get out of here."

Running for their lives for the last two years had kept them fit, and all three were able to maintain a steady pace as they jogged past the village school and over the bridge that led them into Blarney. But Maddy panicked as she saw lights on in some of the houses and a dog began to bark.

"They know we're here!" she yelled. She put on a burst of speed until all three of them were sprinting through the parking lot of Blarney Castle, their breathing ragged as they pulled themselves through the familiar gap in the fence hidden by bushes, and still they raced on, over the footbridge that spanned the chuckling stream, onto the smooth concrete path that led straight to the forbidding medieval castle and past it, to the low tunnel that led to the landscaped gardens and the mound.

Maddy didn't dare look back as her breath caught in her chest and her lungs began to burn with the effort of running. She could taste copper in her mouth and her legs felt heavy but still she ran on, her feet slipping a little on the pebbly paths of the rocky close, the earth and stones dry and loose. Every time she stumbled, her heart went into her mouth and her body tensed for a fall, but she managed to keep on her feet. She knew Danny and Roisin were still running with her, because she could hear the sound of their sneakers hitting the earth and their panting, which seemed increasingly wheezy, but she didn't have the strength to turn her head to look at them. She kept her eyes fixed on the tiny moonlit path that led them straight to the mound and kept going.

She didn't know what she had been expecting as she stumbled up to the mound itself, exhausted. She knew the boundary between the faerie world and the mortal one was really only at its weakest at Halloween, but she had hoped, with all the weird stuff that was going on, that the mound would be reacting in some way.

But it wasn't. It lay there in the moonlight, as peaceful and unremarkable as any other grassy hillock. There was no yawning opening into its depths, no pitch torches smoking greasily in their metal brackets, no faerie guide, and, most important no way in.

"Oh, COME ON!" screamed Maddy in frustration as she sank to her knees and beat at the ground with her fists. "This is not happening, not tonight!"

They all froze and stared at each other as the faint sound of baying dogs drifted toward them on the night air.

"Dogs!" gasped Roisin, her eyes round with fear. "They've got dogs looking for us!"

"Granda wouldn't let them do that," said Danny. "Would he?"

"Maybe it's not Granda who's looking for us," said Maddy.

"We need to get into that mound right now!" said Danny.

"I know!" said Maddy.

"Ro, how do you get into a mound again?" asked Danny, as the sound of the dogs grew louder.

Roisin rubbed at her forehead with her fingertips. "Um, let me think. You can fall asleep and enter through your dreams—"

"Not going to happen," said Maddy.

"The only other way I can think of is spilling the blood of an innocent so you can summon a faerie guide."

"How long is it going to take a guide to get here?" asked Danny.

"No idea, but unless we feel like outrunning those dogs, it's the only chance we've got," said Maddy. She put her hand in her pocket and pulled open the Velcro to get at the iron knife she had hidden in the lining of her jacket. "Right, who's volunteering?"

They all looked at each other, calculating who was the most innocent. Maddy thought of Bang Bang, blood drying on his cracked lips as he died. A blush flooded her cheeks. It wasn't going to be her.

"Ro, it has to be you," said Danny.

"Why? What have you done that disqualifies you?" she asked, her voice squeaky with fear.

Gently, Maddy took her cousin's wrist and turned her hand until the palm faced up. "I only need a couple of drops, Ro," she said. "It won't hurt much." She put the sharp edge of the blade to Roisin's skin and Roisin screwed her eyes shut in anticipation, just as a white stag came bounding up to the mound, gravel spraying from his hoofs as he ran, twin moons floating in his eyes. Maddy and Roisin had just enough time to spring apart as the huge animal leaped between them toward the mound, his snow-white coat burning with an alien intensity in the moonlight, his full spread of antlers curving in front of him as he lowered his head and dived straight into the opening that appeared as the mound shuddered open. Seconds later a quick, silver streak of gray ran in the stag's path and leaped for the same opening, as the beams of powerful flashlights stabbed at the sky and the baying of the hunting dogs echoed loud through the gardens.

"Nero!" screamed Roisin as she recognized the lean wolf and ran after him. Maddy and Danny raced after her, making it into the mound just before it shivered itself closed again. Once inside, torches flared to life against walls of smooth packed earth. She could hear the hoof beats of the stag as it ran on, but Nero was flattened against one wall, panting with exhaustion. His eyes gleamed turquoise in the dim light and his coat was matted with mud and tangled with twigs. His normally glossy silver-gray pelt was dull, and his ribs were showing. Between long yellow teeth, his red tongue flopped out and his eyes stared at them without any sign of recognition.

"Oh, you poor boy," said Roisin, stepping toward the wolf with her hand outstretched. Nero peeled back his black lips and growled at her, although the growl was half a whine of fear. Startled, Roisin jumped back and snatched her fingers out of reach.

"They're more wolfy our side, remember?" said Maddy softly. "Let him go on ahead. He'll remember who we are once he gets to Tír na nÓg."

The wolf stared back at them, terrified, and took a tentative step forward with one of his massive paws. When he saw they were making no move toward him, he bolted through the tunnel and disappeared into the gloom, his plumed tail tucked between his legs.

"Right," said Danny. "Let's get moving. I don't feel like getting stuck in here. I didn't pack enough Mars bars."

Maddy squared her shoulders as they walked through the mound, across its domed main chamber and down another small tunnel that would lead them out into Tír na nÓg.

It won't be so bad this time, she thought. *I'm the Hound of Ireland with the whole might of the Autumn Court behind me, and I've got Danny and Roisin. And I know what to expect this time when I get to the other side.*

But as they emerged from the mound, she heard Danny and Roisin gasp with shock and horror. As she stared at the scene that greeted her, she realized that she really didn't know what to expect at all.

chapter seven

"WHAT THE HELL HAPPENED HERE?" ASKED DANNY. They had expected to step out of the mound into a meadow strewn with wild flowers rolling down a hill before giving way to a forest beneath a crystal-clear sky. Instead, the ground they stood on was scorched to bare earth and the forest had been devastated by fire. The oldest, strongest trees stood charred and blackened, while the younger ones were burned down to the trunks or gone altogether, judging by the clearings that pocked the forest. The sun was rising in the sky but its golden rays struggled to pierce the layer of woodsmoke and no birds sang to welcome it. The cousins were looking at a funeral pyre, the dryads silenced, the animals and birds of the forest fled.

The stag was standing a few feet away, nostrils flaring and collapsing as he breathed deeply. As Maddy watched, he reared up onto his hind legs and transformed into an antlered man, with a cloak made of a patchwork of animal skins falling away from his shoulders to skim the charcoaled ground. He radiated a dark light that pulsed and shifted like an imploding star, his face wreathed in shadows that even the dawn sun could not penetrate. The moons had disappeared from his eyes—now, when he looked at them, his pupils were full of the white light of wheeling stars.

"Cernunnos," said Maddy, "who did this?"

One of the oldest of the Tuatha de Dannan and the Lord of the Forest, Cernunnos cocked his massive head at them, a head that should not have been able to support the weight of that huge spread of antlers. "War has finally come to Tír na nÓg," he said. "The Winter Queen has struck the first blow."

"Liadan," said Danny. He wrinkled his face in disgust and spat on the ground. "I knew it!"

"Weren't you able to stop this?" asked Roisin. "I thought that was the whole point of tying the Winter Queen to you in marriage—so she would not be able to harm the forest. Can't you do anything when your wife goes on the rampage?"

"War changes the pieces on the board," said Cernunnos. "Changes their positions, changes their values. Yes, I should have stopped her. But I didn't get here quick enough. Now the deed is done and events have moved on without me. I have another role to fulfill."

"We can still stop this," said Maddy. "You've left the mortal world, and now you can help us. Now the courts are moving against each other, there is no point in your staying neutral. You're the oldest of the Tuatha; the only other that compares to you is the Morrighan, the High Queen, and she never wakes up! Stop Liadan in her tracks and this will all go away."

"Things have gone too far for that, little Hound," said Cernunnos. "I'm another pawn on the board whose role has changed, and you and I are no longer on the same side. For now I will let you go in peace, but be warned—if we meet again it will not go the same way for you. You've caused a lot of trouble, for just one small girl." With that, he gathered his cloak around himself and strode off into the devastated forest, heading for the Winter Queen's white tower, hidden from view by the pall of gray smoke.

"No longer on the same side?" Maddy yelled at his back. "What does that even mean?"

A wet nose nuzzled at her hand and Maddy looked down to find herself gazing into Nero's yellow eyes. "What is going on around here?" she asked. "Is the pack safe?"

"They went to ground when Liadan got Fenris," said Nero. "I came looking for you. The mound was open—I think Liadan must have made sure of it. She wanted to lure you in."

"What do you mean, she got Fenris?" asked Danny.

"She summoned him to the tower," said Nero. "Didn't say why. But Fenris knew it couldn't be good—it never is when faeries notice wolves. So he told the pack to hide deep in the forest and to keep the pups safe. But he didn't come out again. Raiding parties of elves came out instead and started to slash and burn at the forest. They killed any dryads that tried to stop them, and none of the Tuatha courts arrived to stand in their way either."

"Is Fenris still alive?" asked Roisin. Maddy could hear the tears in her voice. When they had first entered Tír na nÓg, they had stumbled around helpless and lost. It had been the wolf pack and a little dryad called Fionn who had helped them. Now it seemed the wolves were paying for their kindness.

"I hope so," said Nero. "I hid close to a raiding party and I heard them laughing about him. Liadan has him chained in the great hall of the tower and they say she has pinned his jaws together with a sword so he cannot bite."

"That's disgusting!" said Roisin. "That's . . . that's animal cruelty!"

"They said you would come running when you heard Fenris was in danger," said Nero.

"Is that why you risked coming into Blarney?" Maddy asked. "To make sure I came?"

Nero shook his shaggy head. "No, I wanted you to stay in the mortal world, where you would be safe. Liadan intends to fight to the death this time. Fenris would not have wanted you to die because of him."

Her heart melted and Maddy touched Nero's head gently with the tips of her fingers. "It wouldn't have mattered anyhow, Nero," she said. "Liadan sent the dullahan after me, wanted to make sure that I and the whole of Tír na nÓg knew she is trying to kill me. Now that I am a subject of the Autumn Court, it's an act of war. I was going to end up here whatever you tried to do to stop it."

"Come here to me, Nero," said Roisin. "Let me get some of that junk out of your fur."

The wolf padded over to Roisin and the pair of them sank down to the ground together. He put his head in her lap and closed his eyes with a sigh of contentment as Roisin's deft fingers worked clumps of mud and twigs out of his fur.

"I don't like this," said Danny.

"Do I look like I'm doing cartwheels?" asked Maddy.

"But it's like you said—you were going to end up in here no matter what," said Danny. "Being tied to a Tuatha monarch just seems to make you more vulnerable, not less. And I don't like feeling shoved into a corner."

"Ah, but you know what they say about cornered animals," said Maddy. "They always fight hardest."

"That's because they're desperate, Maddy," said Danny. "I don't think that's a good thing."

"Well, it sounds like the two of you are on track for one of your usual mature, reasonable discussions," said Roisin cheerfully. "Or as I like to call them, arguments." She stood up and Nero climbed to his feet, shaking himself briskly. "Why don't we just keep moving and see what happens?"

"Why?" asked Danny.

"Because that's what we've always done before and it's never failed to get us into a fight," said Roisin. "So I say we head for where all the problems start—Liadan's White Tower."

Roisin walked away down the hill with Nero trotting by her side. Maddy and Danny looked at each other and Maddy shrugged. "She's right. Might as well go and spy on Liadan and see what she's up to."

"It would be nice if, just once, we could have something like a plan," said Danny.

"Never gonna happen," said Maddy cheerfully, as she followed Roisin down the hill.

$\sim$

Any cheerfulness Maddy might have felt, no matter how fleeting, was soon crushed by walking in the stricken forest. She had never been anywhere so quiet. Every living thing had fled or died—not even the buzz of insect wings disturbed the silence. She was almost terrified to walk, cringing at the sounds charred wood made as it collapsed beneath the soles of her sneakers, and she hated the puffs of ash that floated up as they walked.

She could tell by the way Danny and Roisin were wincing that they felt the same way. They could not even see the sky. Everything was covered by a cloud of acrid smoke that hung low enough to drift around her head in tendrils. Spots of soot danced in the air and quickly coated her skin and clothes, while the smoke slipped insidiously into her nostrils and her mouth, drying her eyeballs and making every flickering movement of her eyes feel scratchy. It was not long before all three of them were coughing, their eyes red and streaming. Nero kept pausing to wipe at his face with his foreleg, trying to clear his eyes.

Everything was fragile to the touch. At one point Maddy stumbled and put her hand against a huge oak tree to brace herself. That simple touch caused a chunk of its bark to slough off beneath her fingers and crumble to ash. She looked up at it in horror. Was its dryad, the little faerie that lived in the heart of the tree, still alive, curled up somewhere inside, suffering agonizing burns? Could it speak? Could it still feel anything, even the wound Maddy had just inflicted, or had pain sent its mind to another place? The tree loomed over her, twisted and tortured, and gave no sign it even knew she was there. She dashed tears from her red eyes and kept moving.

After a while they all stopped walking and simply stood and stared at each other.

Roisin took a juddering breath. "I've never been anywhere so . . . so . . ."

"Dead," said Danny. Nero flopped on to his belly, put his head on his paws and whimpered.

"I did this," said Maddy, real tears coursing through the grime on her face. She wiped her cheeks with a filthy hand and simply spread more soot around.

Roisin looked at her, her eyes softening with pity. "No, you didn't."

"Liadan wanted me to come back," said Maddy. "She's torturing Fenris and she burned the forest to make sure that happened. So yes, I did this, it's my fault. How many dryads are dead because of me?"

"She's done this before, Maddy, when she first came to Tír na nÓg, remember?" said Danny. "This is what she revels in, the death and the destruction. You are just an excuse for something she would do sooner or later."

"Danny's right," said Roisin. "What she really wants is a war with the Tuatha, a way to break out from Tír na nÓg and have no restraint on her powers. Coming after you is just a way to make that happen."

"She burned the forest because it's too close to the tower," said Nero.

"What?" asked Maddy.

Nero shrugged. "She's always been frightened of the dryads, though I don't think they ever understood that. So many of them, some working with such powerful trees, all of them solitary faeries owing allegiance to no court. They could have thrown their lot in with any Tuatha and come against her. She didn't want that to happen so she burned them. They will be too weak to do anything to her now."

"So this was just Liadan housekeeping before she started her war," said Roisin.

"But Fachtna spoke about the dryads like they were dirt," said Maddy. "To listen to her, you would have thought she was talking about something she scraped off the bottom of her boots."

"People often show hatred of something they are frightened of, rather than admit they are scared," said Nero.

"The dryads could have fought back, they could have done her some damage," said Danny. "Why didn't they?"

"They've never understood war," said Nero. "They are peaceful creatures who only strike if they are attacked. And they have no idea what it means to work together. They have no concept of being in a pack."

"Poor things," said Maddy, looking at the blackened forest around her.

"They'll survive," said Nero. "The younger ones might have perished, but the older trees will grow new shoots and renew themselves and their dryads will heal along with them."

Maddy thought of Fionn, the beautiful little silver-birch dryad. She and her tree had already survived one burning—had they both survived this?

"What are we supposed to do?" said Roisin. "How are we supposed to fight this?"

"We can't," said Danny. "Not on our own. Liadan has a whole army behind her and, no offense, Maddy, but being the Hound doesn't seem worth much and nor does being part of Meabh's court."

"What's that supposed to mean?" asked Maddy, feeling her temper rise as it so often did with Danny.

Danny made a big show of pretending to think, frowning deeply and tapping at his forehead. "Well, being the Hound hasn't given you any superpowers, unless you count being a faerie magnet, which I don't, by the way, seeing as it utterly ruined *my* life. And as for being the subject of the Autumn Court and under their protection, I don't see any Autumn Tuatha turning up to welcome you home, armed to the teeth with something useful like *big pointy swords*!"

"Why do you do this every time?" asked Maddy while Roisin sighed.

"Do what?" asked Danny.

"Every time we get into trouble, instead of doing or saying anything helpful, you just get really, really snarky and start a fight," said Maddy. "It drives me crazy."

"I'm not starting a fight. I'm just pointing out the obvious," said Danny.

"Yeah? Well, give it a rest," said Maddy. "Or at least say something useful."

They all jumped in fright as Nero sprang to his feet and started barking. Horrified, they watched as three riders on white mounts slipped between the trees to stand in front of them. Their long ears and small, slight build showed they were elves and not Tuatha and therefore they were subjects of the Winter Court.

They looked down on Maddy with beautiful, cruel faces.

"We couldn't help but hear your argument," said a dark-haired elf. He smiled but it didn't reach his eyes, and his teeth looked too big and hungry for his red mouth. "Will we do as a welcoming committee?"

chapter eight

NERO BEGAN TO SNARL AT THE ELVES AND PUFFED his fur up to make his body look twice as big. Maddy watched in horror as the elven mounts snarled back, revealing fangs almost twice as long as Nero's, which looked strange in their horse-like faces. Their red eyes glowed with rage as their taloned paws took a step forward through the charred debris on the forest floor. Instinctively Maddy, Danny, Roisin, and Nero took a step back and huddled together. Maddy gagged as the smell of rotting meat rolled over her face from the closest mount.

"You are a brave doggy, aren't you?" said the dark-haired elf. "We caught one of you the other day. He was brave too, even though it took him such a long time to die."

Nero said nothing, just carried on snarling, but Maddy could hear his growl get deeper. She reached out and put a hand on him to calm him—the elves were trying to make him angry and she didn't want him to do something that would get him killed.

"We didn't think there would be much left in the forest worth hunting," continued the elf. "Yet in two days we find two wolves and a Hound. And as an extra treat, two humans. I normally do not like to hunt children—the chase is over far too quickly and you really do not have the strength to last long once we catch you. But it's been so long since I hunted a human that I'll take what I can get." The other elves laughed.

"Liadan won't like it if you kill me," said Maddy.

"True enough," said the elf cheerfully. "That is a pleasure she wants all to herself. But she said nothing about your companions, so they're fair game."

Roisin whimpered, and Maddy heard Danny curse softly under his breath, his voice high with fear.

"She'll be happier if you bring us all in together," said Maddy, slipping her hand into her pocket and fingering her little iron knife.

The elf smiled again and shook his head. "I don't think so," he said. "I think she will be happy enough with just you, little Hound. That means we can have some fun before we bring you in." All three elves tightened their grip on their reins and licked their lips. The mounts stood up straighter and became more alert as they felt the new tension in their riders' bodies. "You know we like to chase," he said. "So start running. I like a fair fight, so we'll give you a head start."

"If we don't run?" asked Danny.

The elf shrugged. "We'll kill you where you stand. And where is the fun in that?"

As soon as the words left his lips there was a flurry of white behind him and a sword arced through the air, gleaming bright even in the dull smoky light. The dark-haired elf's mount screamed in agony and collapsed to the ground, scrambling desperately with its front paws, its back legs lying limp and useless. Nero leaped at the second mount, going straight for the throat. The beast reared up on its back legs, tumbling its rider to the ground as it tried to rake at Nero's sides with its front talons. But Nero hung close to its chest, twisting in the air as he gripped tight, and the pair of them were soon stained with the mount's blood.

The third rider yelled and spurred his mount forward, straight at Maddy, reaching out a hand to grab her, his lips pulled back from his teeth in a snarl. Maddy slashed at him with her knife, and even though she was reeling to one side to avoid his clutching fingers, she still managed to slice open the skin of his palm. The elf screamed and toppled from the side of his mount, which bolted further into the forest. The stricken rider writhed from side to side, clutching at his hand, the skin turning black around the cut as the iron poisoned him. Steam rose from the wound and the elf's screaming hit higher and higher pitches as the iron ate into his flesh.

Maddy turned and saw the other two elves closing on their attacker, swords drawn. She was seven foot tall, a faerie, as slim as a ballet dancer. Her white hair was stiffened with lime into a Mohawk and her bone-white skin was completely covered in pale gray Celtic tattoos. Muscles rippled through her body as she swung a silver great sword two-handed and her eyes glowed red. Her pale lips bared teeth filed to shark's tips, and smaller silver knives were belted around her narrow hips. When Maddy recognized Fachtna, Liadan's chief, she felt as if she had jumped from the frying pan into the fire.

Danny grabbed her arm. "We need to get out of here, while they're all distracted."

"But why is Fachtna fighting elves?" asked Roisin. "It doesn't make sense—they're on the same side."

"I have no idea, but I'm not sticking around to find out," said Danny. He called over to Nero, who was still worrying at the body of the mount he had attacked, even though the beast now lay completely motionless. "Nero, we need to go. NOW!"

Nero looked up, his face covered in gore, and then he bounded to Roisin's side and pressed close to her legs. Roisin was frozen to the spot as she watched Fachtna and the elves fighting—Danny had to run back and start dragging her to make her move.

But while they were hesitating, they lost their chance to make a run for it. With a flick of her wrist Fachtna spun the sword from the dark-haired elf's hands and opened his forehead with a slice across the skull. As the blood poured down his face, he collapsed to his knees, blinded. Fachtna flung out one sharp elbow into the face of the other elf as he tried to attack her from the side. As he stumbled back, she hooked a foot around his ankles and brought him crashing onto his back. She turned to Maddy, pointed her sword at her face, and hissed, "Don't move," before bending to take the prone elf's sword. He glared up at her.

"You're going to die for this, Fachtna," he said. "Liadan doesn't tolerate traitors."

Fachtna shrugged as she stood over him pointing two swords at his face. "Maybe, maybe not," she said. "A lot of us are going to die soon and perhaps my time is close. But it might not be Liadan who accounts for me in the end." Then she bared her gruesome teeth. "However, if you keep annoying me, I will be happy to dispatch you now."

The elf spat at her. "Go ahead! If you can live with the shame of killing an unarmed foe."

"Oh, I could live with that," said Fachtna, "because I don't really consider you worth calling a foe. Too much bark, nowhere near enough bite. But that doesn't mean you're not useful."

She lunged forward and drove the sword points into the earth, a few fractions of an inch from the elf's handsome face. The blood drained from his cheeks and he cringed as she bent close enough to kiss him. "Listen close and listen well," she said, her deep, gravelly voice a dark undercurrent to the sound of the other elves' whimpering and groaning behind her. "Tell your mistress: my bonds are broken, and now that I have the Hound there's no limit to what I can do to cause her harm." She stood up and wrenched the swords free. "Now go."

He got up and ran, leaving his stricken comrades behind. Fachtna watched with a curled lip as the blood-blinded elf and the one with the injured hand painfully climbed to their feet and staggered away, holding on to each other for support. Keeping their eyes fixed on her, Maddy, Danny, Roisin, and Nero tried to sidle away, clinging together like a parody of a three-legged race. But they couldn't be subtle enough—Fachtna's head whipped around and she raised her sword again and growled, "I said. Don't. Move."

One of the mounts was still alive and, as vicious as it was, Maddy couldn't help but pity it as it moaned softly and paddled at the ground with its paws. With its red eyes half-lidded and its mouth closed it almost looked like a beautiful white horse and not a monstrosity.

"What did you do to it?" she asked Fachtna.

"I cut its hamstrings, so now its back legs are paralyzed," said Fachtna.

Roisin gasped. "That's so cruel!"

Fachtna looked at her and raised an eyebrow. "Better than it being able to turn and claw me open from throat to belly," she said. "And in case any of you wants to come back with a clever remark, just remember they were about to attack you." She pointed at Roisin, Danny, and then Nero. "Not one of you was going to come out of that situation healthy and whole."

The mount let out a long, low moan. "It's suffering," said Danny.

"Yes, it is," said Fachtna, unsheathing a wicked-looking silver hunting knife with a serrated edge.

"What are you doing?!" asked Roisin.

"Putting it out of its misery," said Fachtna as she bent down. They all turned their eyes away quickly just before Fachtna drew the blade across its soft white throat. The beast choked for a moment on its own blood and then died with a sigh.

"So why are you killing elves?" asked Roisin, as Fachtna hunted for a piece of moss or some greenery to wipe the blood from her blade.

"I'd forgotten how many questions you ask, child," said Fachtna. "I'm amazed no one has cut your tongue out yet."

"You've left Liadan, haven't you?" asked Danny.

"We heard that elf call you a traitor," said Maddy, as Fachtna's face set in anger.

"Liadan no longer requires my sword," said Fachtna stiffly. "Since she has declared war, her husband has assumed his place as the leader of her war band and her general, as is his duty."

"Cernunnos?" said Maddy. "Are you trying to tell me that the one Tuatha we thought we could count on to help is now fighting for the enemy?!"

"Well, he's a Tuatha, and under their customs a husband has to fight on behalf of his wife, even if he didn't pick the fight," said Fachtna. "Something he would have known when he married that war-crazed demented little elf."

"*You're* calling *Liadan* war-crazed?" said Maddy.

Fachtna paused in cleaning her blade to glare at her. "I am perfectly sane."

"But we need Cernunnos," said Danny, while Maddy rolled her eyes. "He's the only Tuatha that has ever been on our side, even if he hasn't ever actually been much help."

"We thought he cared about us," said Roisin. "Why did he always spend so much time in the mortal world, living among us, pretending to be one of us, if he didn't like mortals?"

"Well, he doesn't care," said Fachtna, as she ran her hand down her blade to test its edge. "He's not going to do a thing to help you, so you might as well get used to that idea. He's a Tuatha—he's not going to choose you over his own kind. He cannot ignore bonds of marriage and family that existed centuries before any of you were born. And let's not forget that war is a game changer. Now that it is upon us, he has a different role to play. As do I."

"What do you mean?" asked Maddy.

"Well, as fate would have it, I am now the closest thing you've got to a friend, little chicks," said Fachtna, as she smiled her cold, shark's smile.

chapter nine

THEY LOOKED AT FACHTNA OPEN-MOUTHED WHILE she gazed back at them, the smile playing about her bloodless lips. Roisin was the first to break the silence. "We're doomed," she said. Fachtna threw back her head and roared with laughter and they all jumped about a foot backward to get away from her. None of them had ever heard Fachtna laugh before and it was quite scary. They had no idea what it meant when she laughed, and they also got a better view of her hideous teeth, which made Maddy shudder.

"It's really not that bad, little chicks," said Fachtna. "Now you have a friend with a strong sword arm who is not afraid to get into a fight over you. When did Cernunnos ever risk anything on your behalf?"

"See, that's the key word right there, isn't it?" said Maddy. "You're happy to fight 'over' us, not 'for' us or 'with' us."

Fachtna sneered. "You're not good enough to fight with me, and I'm not desperate enough to be a servant and fight for you."

"But you make us sound as if we are things," said Danny. "As if we're prisoners."

Fachtna tutted. "*Prisoners*," she said. "That's such a harsh word."

"So we are free to say, 'Thanks, but no thanks,' to your offer of help and walk off?" asked Roisin.

Fachtna grinned. "Oh no."

"I knew it!" said Danny.

"This is a better offer than you realize," said Fachtna, her face cold and hard now and all pretense at humor gone. "If you thought Tír na nÓg was dangerous before, you have no idea what it is like when it is at war. You've been here five minutes and already you've run into a raiding party that could have killed you or dispatched you back to Liadan. A raiding party, might I add, that was made up of inexperienced young warriors who were easily beaten by one swordswoman."

"How do you know how long we've been in here?" asked Maddy.

"I was tracking you the whole time," said Fachtna. "Not even the wolf spotted me."

Nero had the good grace to look ashamed.

"You won't last any time at all with all four courts on the rampage," said Fachtna. "You need help. I want the

Hound and I am willing to take her useless companions under my protection at the same time, in return for her cooperation. I think that's a good bargain."

"Why do you need me so badly?" asked Maddy, her voice sharp with suspicion.

"I have a plan, little Hound, and you are right at the heart of it," said Fachtna.

"Pray tell," said a familiar voice somewhere above their heads. Startled, they all looked up to see Queen Meabh perched in a tortured tree, its branches raking the sky around her in agony. In a world of black and gray she burned as bright as a ruby. Her red hair tumbled around her like a cloak, thick and heavy and snarled in knots and tangles. Her tall, slim figure was dressed in red plaid, while a gold torc gleamed against her milk-white throat. Gold armbands curved around her muscular biceps and her eyes gleamed fresh and green. She stood up on her perch, held her arms out to her sides, and leaned forward. Everyone except Fachtna yelled as she tipped out into space, expecting her to plummet toward the ground, but instead the Tuatha simply walked down the trunk of the tree, bits of burned bark crumbling at the touch of her leather-booted feet, as if she was out on a stroll. Her familiar, a gigantic black dog with huge yellow eyes called the Pooka, padded toward her as she reached the ground and rubbed himself against her leg.

"Not impressed, Fachtna?" she asked as she rearranged her plaid.

"Not really," said Fachtna. "I've seen that party trick before."

"My, my, my," said Meabh. "How sharp your tongue has grown since you have no monarch to curb it. Did it hurt terribly, Fachtna, to be cast aside for another?"

"I left of my own free will," sneered Fachtna. "It feels good to have it back again."

"Does it really?" said Meabh, circling the war faerie, a little wake of dust stirred by her heavy skirts. "You surprise me—you always struck me as the kind of faerie who likes the leash and chain. But why leave Liadan just as the Winter Queen gives you exactly what you want? All that blood and death and agony—I would have thought you would have been slavering in anticipation and kissing her icy feet for the chance to draw that sword in a proper battle."

She stopped, her blood-red lips inches away from Fachtna's cheek as the faerie stared straight ahead. "Unless, as you say, you have another plan. Something that will deliver you a little more."

She walked around Fachtna and behind Maddy and placed a long, triple-jointed hand on her shoulder. Idly, she picked up a strand of Maddy's wavy brown hair and rubbed it between her fingertips.

"But what puzzles me is why you think you can simply steal what is mine to help you achieve your goals," said Meabh. "You know full well the Hound has sworn allegiance to me. You cannot use one of my subjects for your own ends without asking my permission—nor can she give her services away."

Still Fachtna said nothing.

"But if these plans were to suit my own aims, perhaps I might be persuaded to be generous," said Meabh.

Fachtna's eyes flickered toward her.

"Ah," said Meabh, her lips curving in a sly smile. "Now we are negotiating. You want my little pup here and her feeble companions—to what purpose? What would *you* want, Fachtna, more than anything?" Meabh thought for a moment, drumming her spider fingers on Maddy's shoulder. Maddy swallowed and glanced at Danny and Roisin, who looked back at her with white, worried faces. "Would it have something to do with a traveling island and its sole occupant?"

This time Fachtna looked straight at Meabh and held her gaze, still keeping her white lips firmly clamped together.

"Perhaps you would like to see this occupant meddling in our affairs once more?" said Meabh. "Say I were to help you, send you on your way with some tools necessary for the job and the help of the little Hound here and her friends—what do I get in return?"

"Silence," said Fachtna. "Your subject returned to you. And a debt to be paid."

"That's good enough for me!" said Meabh brightly. "Come, come, let's send you on your way."

And with that she simply walked off, back in the direction they had come from, Fachtna striding behind her.

"What just happened?" asked Maddy.

"It sounds as if we've all been volunteered for something," said Roisin.

"Whatever it is, I bet we're not going to like it," said Danny. "And why couldn't they just come out and say whatever it is Fachtna wants? Why all the cloak-and-dagger stuff?"

"I think I know what they are up to," said Nero. "Fachtna is going to wake the Morrighan."

They all looked at him, hope making their eyes sparkle. Maddy actually felt giddy with relief for the first time in a long time. The Morrighan could finish Liadan once and for all. The High Queen of the Tuatha de Dannan, it was her magic that brought Tír na nÓg into being. She was the channel for all the hopes and dreams of the mortal world, the nightmares, the feelings and thoughts. She used it all to create a magic that kept Tír na nÓg alive and the Tuatha away from the mortal world. She dreamed, and Tír na nÓg thrived. She also had the power to crown and dethrone monarchs and had intervened to put an end to wars in the past. There was no way Liadan could stand against her.

"We've been saying this right from the beginning," said Danny. "Wake the Morrighan up and let her sort the mess out."

"I've heard it's dangerous," said Nero. "There is no telling what the Morrighan will do if she is woken."

"But she wants balance," said Maddy. "She wants Tír na nÓg to carry on as it is, locked away from the mortal world, the four courts balancing each other out, none more powerful than the others. Surely, if Fachtna manages to wake her, all she's going to want to do is put everything back the way it should be. That will mean getting rid of Liadan, seeing as she is determined to mess everything up."

"It sounds like a plan where nothing could go wrong, which really should tell us that it's all going to go *horribly* wrong," said Roisin.

"Do we have any other options?" asked Maddy.

"Do we ever?" said Danny. Roisin sighed.

"Are you coming with us, Nero?" asked Maddy.

"Are you joking? Anywhere near Fachtna is probably the safest place for me to be until this is all over," said the wolf. "Considering Liadan is the only one who ever welcomed us here, Fachtna might still be the safest faerie to be around when this is all over."

"Why does Fachtna need me so much anyway?" asked Maddy as they scurried after the faeries.

"Ritual sacrifice?" suggested Danny. "OW!" he yelled as Maddy and Roisin punched him on both arms.

"That's not funny," said Roisin.

"No, it's really not," said Maddy.

"It's also a really bad guess," called Nero over his shoulder as he loped ahead of them. "Part of the bargain was that Meabh gets Maddy back." He stopped for a second, his brow furrowing. "Mind you, she didn't say whether or not you had to be alive."

"NERO!" yelled Maddy.

"I'm kidding, I'm kidding!" said the wolf as he trotted off with his tail wagging.

They jogged after Nero through the deathly quiet forest. Soon they left its ravaged boundaries to find themselves following Meabh, her Pooka, and Fachtna to the river's edge. Maddy shuddered when she saw who was waiting for them there. Meabh's storm hags, her ladies-in-waiting, three hideous women in greasy gray rags, their scabbed scalps pocked with limp strands of hair, each with one eye gleaming with malevolence in her blue-black face. Two of them carried black bundles in their arms, while the third held a bow made of a pale wood.

Meabh stopped by the river and looked down into the rushing water, dirty and soot-stained as it carried away the wounds of the forest. She reached into her plaid, pulled out a walnut, and cracked it neatly in half along its seam.

"You will need a boat, of course," she said. The half a walnut shell balanced on her open palm and she blew gently on it. It spiraled out of her hand and up into the air, out over the river, where it drifted down to the water. But instead of speeding away with the current, the little shell began to expand as soon as it touched the water and it grew in front of Maddy's amazed eyes until it rocked gently on the water in front of her, a boat big enough for them all.

"You will need fire and iron to hold the place you are going to," continued Meabh, holding out her hands to the storm hags. The one with the smallest bundle stepped forward first and gave it to her. She pulled away the dark cloth to reveal a lantern made of silver, housing a bright-green flame.

"This flame will never go out," warned Meabh as she handed it to Fachtna. "Never let it out of your sight and be careful where you set it down." She turned again to the storm hags and clicked her fingers. "Arrows with iron heads, coated with pitch. Be careful not to cut yourself." Maddy noticed she left the arrows covered in their thick black cloth, and that Fachtna shuddered as she took the bundle in her arms.

"You keep iron?" asked Maddy.

"Yes," said Meabh.

"Why on earth would you keep something so dangerous to yourself?" asked Roisin.

"Humans do the same thing," said Meabh. "You stockpile weapons, create new ones that kill long after they have been used. Why did humans create the atom bomb when they knew it could be a planet killer? And yet you created it, built it, and mass-produced it, and enemies sold it to enemies. My keeping a bit of iron hardly compares, wouldn't you say?"

"How do you know so much about us?" asked Danny.

"When other faeries cavort and hunt in the mortal world on Halloween night, I watch TV," said Meabh, shrugging.

"Really?" asked Roisin.

"Yes. It's quite interesting," said Meabh.

"What's your favorite show?" asked Danny.

Roisin and Maddy stared at Danny in horror, while Meabh simply raised an eyebrow at him. One of the storm hags snickered but was silenced with an elbow to the ribs by one of her sisters.

Fachtna cleared her throat. "With respect, Queen Meabh, time is wasting. The Winter Court is preparing to march to war and will be ready any day now."

"Of course, of course," said Meabh, waving them away with a languid sweep of her long hand. They clambered awkwardly into the boat, which bobbed about on the spot without an anchor. Maddy thought it was going to capsize when Nero jumped in, it lurched so violently, but it managed to stay afloat. As soon as they were all in, it began to float downstream.

"We've no oars!" cried Roisin, peering over the rim of the walnut shell at Meabh.

"They're pointless when you don't know where you are going," said Meabh as she began to walk away, covering her bright red hair and her plaid with a gray cloak. "Cheer up, Maddy," she called back over her shoulder. "Soon armies will clash, the Hound will run, and we will have a resolution to so many problems."

The storm hags cackled as they followed their queen. Only the Pooka was left on the riverbank, staring at Maddy with his glowing yellow eyes.

Maddy watched Meabh stride away with the burned, smoldering forest in the background, smoke obscuring everything but the devastation.

chapter ten

"'WHAT'S YOUR FAVORITE SHOW?!'" SAID ROISIN TO Danny. "You're standing in front of the witch queen and *that's* what you ask her? I'm amazed she didn't turn you into a frog!"

"I couldn't help it!" said Danny. "I mean, there she is, standing there looking all medieval, going on about the TV. You're telling me you didn't want to know? What if she said it was *The X Factor*?"

They looked at each other and burst out laughing, with Nero wagging his tail and looking from face to face.

"What's *The X Factor*?" he asked.

"Trust me, you don't want to know," said Roisin, giggling and draping an arm around him. He snuggled close to her.

"I don't think that was the right question though," said Maddy.

"How do you mean?" asked Danny.

"You've got to be careful about the questions you ask faeries," said Maddy. "They can't lie, but that doesn't mean they can't avoid telling you the truth. You asked her what her favorite show was—you should have asked her *why* she was watching TV."

Roisin's smile slipped off her face and she frowned. "It's a bit creepy, isn't it?"

Maddy nodded.

"Why?" said Danny. "TV is great—of course she'd be curious if she knew about it."

"But that's just the thing, Danny," said Maddy. "The Tuatha are not curious about us; we're nothing—'mud people' according to Cernunnos, remember? So why would Meabh watch TV?"

"It doesn't sound like she's watching reality TV either," said Roisin. "From what she said, newscasts are more her kind of thing."

"So she's learning about us," said Maddy. "How we are now."

Roisin shuddered.

"So?" said Danny.

"I don't know," said Maddy. "I don't know what it means, but with Meabh it's never good."

They drifted along in silence for a while. The sides of the walnut shell were high and it was an effort to stand up and see out. As they bobbed and twirled and raced ever faster with the strengthening current, it felt too dangerous to try to stand. So they huddled in the bottom of the bowl and tried to get as comfortable as they could on the ridged, sloping surface.

"So are we going to Hy Breasail then?" Maddy asked Fachtna, who had huddled as far from them as she could, her long limbs folded around her. The war faerie was leaning back and looking up at the morning sky, her red eyes pale in the sunlight.

"Yes, little Hound, we are going to find Hy Breasail," said Fachtna. "And we will wake the Morrighan."

"What's Hy Breasail?" asked Danny.

"The floating island where the Morrighan sleeps," said Roisin. "We did these stories in school. Did you not pay attention?"

"No, I was scared I might learn something," said Danny.

Maddy ignored them and addressed Fachtna. "So why couldn't you just say that to Meabh? Why all the talking in code?" she asked.

Fachtna sighed. "Why must you always answer with questions?" she said wearily. "Why do you even have to ask questions in the first place? Is it not obvious?"

"No," said Maddy stubbornly.

"Fine," said Fachtna. She glared at them all and her blood-red eyes seemed to glow in the shade of the walnut shell. She looked more than a little demonic and Maddy swallowed and half wished she had kept her mouth shut.

"Meabh can't lie, as you have already pointed out," she said. "But it seems to suit her that the Morrighan is woken. However, it might not suit all her fellow monarchs and they might be angry if they knew she had a hand in helping me. If we didn't have a conversation about it, then she can deny ever talking about it with me. She can say, with all honesty, that I never told her what I was going to do and she never thought to ask. It makes it harder for Spring or Summer to hold her responsible for whatever happens next."

"What will happen next?" asked Roisin.

"A quick start to this war, and a swift end to it as well," said Fachtna. "If we can get the Morrighan to move against Liadan, the Winter Court will be crushed. And instead of enduring years of petty battles while the other Tuatha squabble over Winter's crown, the Morrighan can award it to whoever she thinks fit to wear it."

"*That's* why you want to wake the Morrighan!" said Roisin. "You want to be the next Winter Queen."

They stared at her in disbelief, while Fachtna's wings rattled with anger.

"Are you insane?" asked Danny.

"I think I have already explained that I am not," said Fachtna, her voice icy.

"Doesn't mean you're right," said Danny.

"I wouldn't argue with the one who has *all* the weapons," said Fachtna.

"He has a point, Fachtna," said Maddy. "You're not a Tuatha."

"Nor is Liadan," said Fachtna.

"Exactly. Look at what the Winter crown has done to her," said Maddy. "You know if you become the Winter monarch you have to wear Winter's cold all the time, even if you take the crown off. Only the Tuatha are strong enough to do that—Liadan thought she was old enough and powerful enough to do what they do, but instead it's warped her body and her mind." Maddy shuddered as she thought of Liadan's white eyes, that had been boiled with the cold inside her until only a smudge of color remained, a thumbprint of gray as a reminder of what once had been blue. "She's insane, Fachtna. Do you really want that to be your fate?"

"No one says it has to be," said Fachtna.

Maddy opened her mouth to carry on arguing but Fachtna lost her patience. "Enough!"

They were all quiet for a moment until Danny piped up, "So how can we find Hy Breasail if we don't know where it is?"

Fachtna roared with impatience. "This is the last question I will answer and then we will play the no-talking game," she said. "The rules are: the next person to speak before I do loses their tongue and I get to keep it! Understood?"

They nodded at her dumbly.

"The island of Hy Breasail is not anchored to any-thing," she explained. "It drifts on the surface of the sea. We cannot find it if we search for it—it is a thing that can only be seen from the corner of one's eye. So we drift that we may happen upon it, and when we do, we can secure it with fire and iron, hence the lantern and the iron-tipped arrows. But do not be under any illusions that we are waking a sleeping beauty. Your people worshipped her as the triple-faced goddess: the maiden, the mother, and the hag. But she was also known as the Scauld Crow, because she took such an interest in war. It's the Morrighan who can decide who wins or loses a battle, who wears the crown, or who loses their head. Now be quiet or I will behead all of you!"

chapter eleven

COWED BY FACHTNA'S FIERCE GLARES, AND THE
way she started twirling a knife between her long fingers, Maddy decided to keep quiet and ask no more
questions. She huddled with Danny, Roisin and Nero
as far away from the faerie as they could get, and rummaged through the knapsacks for food.

Danny certainly had not been thinking about a
balanced diet when he packed. The food consisted of
chocolate, chips and cookies. Still, it was food and they
shared what they had with Nero, who gobbled everything
down so fast it looked as if it didn't even touch the sides.
Exhausted from a long night, they were rocked to sleep by
the waves, bathed in the warm rays of the summer sun.

It was almost dark when Maddy woke up and it took
her a second to register where she was. It took another

second for her to notice the thick fog drifting around the boat. She jerked upright in a panic, forgetting where she was. Fachtna clamped a hand over her mouth to stifle her scream and held her steady.

"Be easy," she hissed. "It's a sea fog, nothing more. We're a long way from the Shadowlands now."

Last year Maddy had been forced to journey into the Shadowlands, the stronghold of a race of warlocks called the Coranied. Hated by humans and faerie folk alike, they were granted sanctuary by the Morrighan because they had a unique gift. The Coranied were able to harvest all the dreams and emotions of human beings and channel them to the Morrighan. They were the ones who provided her with the building blocks to create Tír na nÓg and they helped her control it. The Morrighan kept a tight hold on Tír na nÓg. She wanted peace, and each of the four Tuatha courts was a balance, a block to the others' bid for power. But war could disrupt that balance and break the Morrighan's grip. The last war between the Tuatha had been sparked by the disappearance of the previous Winter Queen. Liadan, escaping the mortal world's cold north with her band of elves, had used the chaos to grab the Winter crown for herself. So far, no Tuatha monarch trusted any of the others enough to try to unite to overthrow Liadan, and Liadan herself would not communicate with the other courts. So again the Morrighan kept her balance and peace was restored.

The Shadowlands were permanently covered by a mist of dreams. All human dreams, hopes, fears, the darkest desires, the most frightening nightmares seeped into Tír na nÓg like a pollution, distilled down by the Coranied in their cauldrons as food for the faeries. And there were things living in that mist. Maddy shuddered at the memory. When a mortal has a near-death experience in Tír na nÓg, they leave a bit of themselves behind. They seem to hold on to a sense of themselves and they gather in the mist, listening to the Coranied at their work and to the whispers of humankind in the cauldrons. The mist had been full of the tortured splinters of human souls, cut off from the mortal world and the humans they belonged to, doomed to wander forever in the limbo of the Shadowlands. Maddy woke up at night, screaming and twisting in sweat-soaked sheets as she remembered the hatred and the anger, the longing and the desperation in those split souls in that mist.

And how they hated Maddy! She remembered a tortured, wizened thing screaming at her as it clawed her arm. *What good is a Hound who leaves us to suffer? What good is a hero who doesn't come to the rescue?*

Even faerie kind were terrified of the mist of dreams. Only Meabh would walk in the lands of the Coranied.

"It's only sea fog," repeated Fachtna as she lowered her glowing red orbs to Maddy's wide and terrified eyes. "Only sea fog," she said again, her voice gentle.

Surprised at her tone, Maddy stared back at her and gradually her heart stopped racing, her breathing slowed and she relaxed.

Fachtna nodded her approval. "Good. I don't want you capsizing this thing and drowning us all."

But Maddy stiffened as a new sensation caused her skin to tingle. Fachtna's head snapped up as she sniffed at the air, and Roisin, Danny, and Nero jerked awake.

"What is that?" asked Danny as Nero began to yip in excitement.

It was as if they had drifted close to a massive battery. Maddy still couldn't see anything in the pillowy fog, but there was a throbbing noise at the edge of her senses as if from an engine miles underground. Her hair lifted and curled in a haze of static and her mouth tasted of metal.

"Hy Breasail!" said Fachtna. "The source of power. Hand me those arrows!" she barked at Maddy, pointing to the bundle on the floor of the boat. Maddy bent carefully to avoid rocking the shell too much and untied the bundle with shaking fingers. Fachtna unwrapped the lantern of green witch-fire and held her hand out. Maddy noticed her fingers jerked back ever so slightly as Maddy placed the smooth wooden shaft of an arrow in her palm—her instincts were probably telling her to shy away from the metal that could poison her. She held the arrowhead in the lantern until the pitch coating the iron caught fire, notched the arrow to her bow and let loose.

The brightly burning arrow flared in the mist but was quickly lost to sight. Maddy could hear the splash and sizzle as it fell into the sea, the sounds amplified by the fog until it seemed as if the arrow had fallen only a few inches away. A second later, something big bumped against the bottom of the shell.

"What was that?" asked Roisin, her voice trembling with fear as Nero began to bark.

"Keep quiet, you stupid animal!" said Fachtna. "Another," she said to Maddy, and Maddy wordlessly passed her a second arrow. Again Fachtna lit the tip and again she fired it into the mist. Again the arrow fell sizzling into the sea. Maddy held her breath.

This time, whatever was beneath the boat hit it hard enough to make it tip. Roisin screamed as water slopped over the sides and Nero started up a volley of barking.

"Be quiet or I'll throw you overboard!" Fachtna roared. "Arrow!"

In her fear, Maddy dropped the bundle at her feet and Fachtna yelped and fell back against the shell wall as the iron heads rolled toward her feet. This probably saved her life as the next collision hit the boat so hard it lifted out of the water. If Fachtna had been standing, she would have been thrown over the side. Another collision came just seconds later and Fachtna screamed with them as the boat spun in a giddy circle.

"You," said Fachtna, pointing at Roisin. "Do something!"

"What am I supposed to do?" asked Roisin, sobbing with terror.

"You can manipulate the magic of this place. I know you can," said Fachtna. "Do it now, before we all die!"

It was as if a lightbulb went off in Maddy's head. "Ro, remember the nightmares, the horses you just imagined into being and the way you made them from shadows? Do it again!"

"What, make horses?" asked Roisin as another thud made them all scream.

"No, an engine, Ro. Make an engine!" screamed Danny.

"OK, let me think," said Roisin as she gripped the edge of the shell and peeped over the side. "Fachtna, there's lots of things in the water—big things!"

Another impact sent the shell spinning again and Danny had to lunge forward and grab Roisin's legs before she went overboard. Nero lay flat and covered his eyes with his paws.

"We already know that!" screamed Maddy. "Do something, Ro, please!"

She heard Roisin muttering away to herself and then the shell tipped, ever so slightly, and began to rush through the water like a speedboat. Maddy peered cautiously over the side and could see white plumes of water spraying around from the shell as it cut through the waves.

"It's working!" she yelled.

"Can you see anything?" called Fachtna over the hiss of the water.

Dark shapes were breaking the surface to gleam like pearls in the moonlight before sinking back down. Lots of shapes, lots of pearls.

Maddy swallowed. "Whatever they are, they're still with us!"

Fachtna snarled and scrambled for one of the arrows that were rolling around the floor of the shell. She lit and fired and still it fell short of Hy Breasail. They couldn't be far from it. Maddy could feel the power of the place clamping down on her head, squeezing her skull until it hurt. If only they could see it through the fog!

Fachtna screamed with frustration, spun in the shell with a flaming arrow notched to her bow and let loose without taking aim. Maddy waited to see the green fire drop and to hear the splash and hiss as the arrow burned out in the sea. But this flame caught and held, flaring like a beacon in the mist on the right-hand side of the shell.

"Turn us around," yelled Fachtna to Roisin. She pointed at the flame. "Bring us to that light!"

Rosin turned her brown eyes to the flame and stared at it without blinking. The shell turned with her head and began to speed up, so much so that the breeze its passage created whipped Maddy's hair back from her face. Something dark was beginning to take shape in the fog, something that reared up high above her head. As the fog gave way in ragged tendrils Maddy could see an island rising up from the water.

It balanced on foundations that narrowed to a dagger point, the island spreading as it grew farther out of the sea. It should have been physically impossible, but not only was this island still upright, a jet-black castle grew with it, rock and building twined together seamlessly, not an inch of land left around the castle even to provide a path. It was as if the castle had been carved from the island. Its obsidian walls were set with arched windows whose panes glittered in the moonlight and a single tower grew from the roof of the castle, pointing like a finger into the night sky.

"There's no way in!" yelled Danny. "There is no way onto that island unless we climb."

"Or fly," said Fachtna calmly. She looked at Maddy. "I could carry you."

Maddy scrambled back from the edge of the shell and entwined her arms with Danny's and Roisin's. "I'm not leaving them behind," she said, as another thud pushed the shell forward. "Find a proper way in or we are getting out of here."

"Fine!" spat Fachtna. "Bring us around the island. There has to be a way in."

The boat moved off to the left, and as they began to edge around the island Maddy spotted something.

"Stairs!" she cried. Black steps rose from a small jetty to an opening cut into the rock. Roisin aimed for the jetty—a little too enthusiastically. The shell crashed into the side and splintered, ice-cold seawater pouring in through the breach.

"Abandon ship!" cried Nero, leaping from the boat, his claws scrambling for purchase on the rock as he landed awkwardly on the jetty.

Fachtna held up the lantern of witch-fire as Maddy, Danny, and Roisin clambered over the side of the wildly rocking shell and onto solid rock. Another crash saw a hole torn open in the shell, and as it began to sink, Fachtna lost her balance and tipped over the side.

Maddy yelled as the war faerie's head went under, and when she bobbed back into view, coughing and spluttering, she grabbed at the faerie's wrist, which was still holding the burning lantern, and towed her toward the jetty. Fachtna looked up into her face, her white hair plastered to her skull, and then she screamed in pain. Maddy started to drag her from the water and as the faerie got a better grip, she hauled herself onto the pier. There was a massive bite mark on her calf and it was bleeding freely. Maddy peered over the side to see what had caused it and a sleek, elegant head rose out of the water and gazed at her with huge brown eyes.

Seals? she thought, as the animal bared its huge fangs at her. Then two large webbed hands slipped out of the water and gripped the edge of the jetty, and a man's face, framed by dark, dripping hair began to emerge. He hissed at Maddy, showing her fangs at least as big as the seal's.

"Selkies!" yelled Danny.

Fachtna pushed Maddy away from her and toward the stairs. "Run!"

They raced for the slippery stone stairs, Fachtna limping along behind them. Maddy forced herself not to look down to the surf that crashed against the rock beneath her, or to think about how the steps had no handrail as she climbed. They all raced through the small, dark opening cut into the rock, and Danny found a stone door open in the wall. He began to force it shut as Maddy and Fachtna ran through, its hinges squealing in protest. Maddy turned to see the selkie running up the stairs behind them, webbed feet slapping awkwardly on the stone steps, eyes burning with anger. She and Fachtna threw their weight behind the door and helped Danny slam it closed just as the selkie reached the top of the steps. Fachtna rammed the bolt home as his body slammed into it, making the tunnel boom. They could hear the creature raging outside as he threw his weight against the door and the *slap, slap, slap* of other webbed feet as they rushed to join him.

Fachtna gripped Maddy's shoulder and squeezed.

"Good girl," she said, her voice soft. "That was bravely done."

Maddy's head flew up in shock as she looked into Fachtna's red eyes and the tunnel echoed to the sound of the selkies' rage.

chapter twelve

"WHY ARE THE SELKIES TRYING TO ATTACK US?" asked Danny as they made their way up the narrow staircase to the castle above. "I thought they didn't care what the Tuatha got up to."

The selkies were solitary faeries, owing allegiance to no court. They kept themselves aloof from the power games in Tír na nÓg. Maddy was as shocked as Danny that they had tried so hard to kill them.

"They really, really don't want us to wake the Morrighan, do they?" asked Roisin.

"I don't really care what a bunch of primitive faeries think," snarled Fachtna, all softness gone. "Keep moving."

"Charming," muttered Roisin as they climbed on, the green witch-fire making the walls dance as its flame flickered. The booming sound of the selkies trying to break through the door began to grow quieter. Maddy had to admire their stubbornness.

As they climbed farther from the sea, the air became staler. The top of the stairs was sealed by a black stone door carved all over with writhing dragons, their sinuous bodies creating a lattice of serpents as their jaws gaped. Maddy's flesh crawled to look at it. All it needed was a sign nailed above it saying "Abandon Hope, All Ye Who Enter."

There was no lock or handle. Roisin pressed her palms to the stone and found the door swung open easily at her touch. It opened on to an inky, echoing darkness. Nero cautiously stretched his neck just past the frame and sniffed the air.

"Ugh," he sneezed. "It smells like a tomb in there."

"You know, considering she is the center of power in Tír na nÓg, the Morrighan is surprisingly vulnerable," said Roisin nervously. "No locks, no guards—there's no sign that anyone is even alive in here."

"She's not guarded because no one dares come near her, do they?" Danny said to Fachtna. "It's too dangerous to come here, isn't it?"

"Keep moving," said Fachtna, her rough voice low and full of menace.

Danny shook his head. "We need to think about this." He turned to Maddy. "I know you think waking the Morrighan is going to be the answer to all our problems, but maybe there is another way we haven't thought of. With three courts against one, I don't see how we could lose against Liadan anyway, even without the Morrighan."

"It's not about beating her with sheer numbers, Danny, it's about stopping another war starting over the Winter crown," said Maddy. "A war like that could go on for years and we'll still be in the firing line if courts keep coming after me to tip the balance. They don't care about hurting everyone around me. The Morrighan can award the crown to whoever she chooses, and the Tuatha will not argue with her decision. I only pledged allegiance for a thousand days, remember? In just over two years I'll be free of the Autumn Court and we can have a normal life. I need to buy time."

"Yeah, but do you really want to risk dying so Fachtna can be the next Winter Queen?"

Fachtna grabbed Danny by the arm and flung him into the shadows. Roisin and Maddy screamed as the darkness swallowed him whole and then they heard him shouting, "What I am lying on? WHAT AM I LYING ON?"

Fachtna stepped over the threshold and held the lantern high. The green flame flared and illuminated a great hall, its vaulted ceiling stretching far above their heads. High above them, weak moonlight crept in through the arched cathedral windows. The walls were covered in banners and tapestries, their imagery vague and ghostly behind a thick layer of dust. Huge wooden chandeliers hung from the beams suspended by chains black with age and dirt. Their round rims were studded with massive candles as long and as thick as Maddy's arm, but long gray webs hung from them like rags, floating in the draft from the open door. Fachtna aimed the lantern at Danny and it was only then that Maddy realized what he was thrashing around in.

Bones.

The floor was white with them, a jumble of skeletons. Maddy looked around and saw the long thin skull of a Tuatha, a huge broad skull with curving tusks that could only be a troll, small ones with fangs, others with rounded bones and short blunt teeth. She even thought she saw skulls that looked uncomfortably human. As she walked toward Danny her feet crunched over splinters and fragments of bone, stirred up dust from bones long ground down to powder and kicked aside legs and arms, shoulder blades, stepped around ribcages, almost lost her footing altogether as tiny finger bones and knuckles rolled beneath the rubber soles of her sneakers.

She closed her lips tightly against the dust that rose up around her plodding feet and concentrated on Danny as he got up, spitting and pawing at his tongue to get the dust out of his mouth. He beat frantically at his clothes, raising a white cloud of ground bone.

"What happened here?" he asked.

Fachtna raised the lantern higher. "Perhaps they were waiting for her to wake up."

Toward the back of the room there was a dais. But instead of a throne, a carved wooden four-poster bed was placed in the middle of it. It was shrouded in black gauze, yards and yards of the stuff, looped and folded until the fabric became opaque with all the dense layering, hiding the bed within. Fachtna's red orbs began to glow with excitement as she strode across the hall, kicking bones out of her way as she went. Maddy, Danny, Roisin, and Nero hurried after her on the path she created and crowded behind her as she slashed at the gauze with her silver sword, tearing it down from the posts and sending up a cloud of dust that had them all coughing and spluttering.

"At last," whispered Fachtna as they looked down on the figure lying on the bed.

It was a Tuatha, Maddy could tell from the height of the figure and the length of her bones. But it was unlike any Tuatha Maddy had ever met. Its strangely lumpy face was covered with a fine black veil. Long, wavy black hair poured like a river over the dusty pillow and overflowed the mattress to puddle on the floor. The long, triple-jointed toes were tipped with hard black nails that had grown so long they had curved in on themselves many times, spooling around and around and around into little spirals. But what was really unusual were the huge black wings that enfolded the figure from neck to ankle, crossing neatly at the ends so their tips pointed in opposite directions. The smooth feathers shone with a deep gloss, radiating life and health in the light of the lantern.

"The Morrighan?" asked Maddy.

Fachtna nodded, her eyes never leaving the figure on the bed.

"What's that?" asked Roisin, pointing to a tarnished silver shape suspended over the Morrighan's face from the wooden frame of her bed.

Danny reached over and pulled it toward him on its chain. "It's a funnel," he said. "Who has a funnel dangling over their face?"

"It's to wake her up," said Fachtna, looking at Maddy in a way she really didn't like.

"OK," said Danny. "And how does it do that? Are we supposed to poke her with it?"

"NO!" snapped Fachtna, her eyes flying to his face.

Danny let go of the silver funnel as if it had burned him, and it swung wildly from side to side on its chain. He held his hands up in the air. "I'm joking!"

"Well, don't," said Fachtna. Her eyes returned to Maddy's face. "She needs a sacrifice to wake her up, an offering."

"Let me guess," said Maddy, her stomach clenching. "Blood?"

Fachtna nodded. "It's why I need you. She has been asleep so long I don't even know if she will wake. But the blood of a Hound is potent . . ."

"If I do this for you, Fachtna, you have to promise me something," said Maddy.

"Anything," breathed Fachtna, her eyes glowing. "Name it."

"Once you are Winter Queen, and assuming we all get out of this alive, your court has to leave us alone. Your court has to leave all mortals alone."

"Done," said Fachtna.

"And you have to protect us and our family against any comeback from the Spring and Summer Courts. I'll handle Autumn myself. The wolf pack will also remain under the protection of the Winter Court."

"I swear it," said Fachtna. "On my life, you, the wolves, and all you love will be protected by my court."

"And your court leaves all mortals alone, even on Halloween?"

"I swear it," said Fachtna.

"Good," said Maddy. She shrugged her jacket off, rolled up her sleeve, and held out her arm, the soft white underside up. "Let's get on with it then."

"Maddy . . ." said Danny, a warning in his voice.

"It's a good deal," said Maddy, her eyes never leaving Fachtna's. "I'm taking it."

The faerie sheathed her sword and put the lantern on the ground. She pulled a small dagger from the strap around her chest and put the tip against Maddy's flesh. Maddy uttered a hiss of pain through clenched teeth as Fachtna drew the blade along her arm. Nero whimpered as Maddy's blood welled up in the wound. Fachtna grabbed the silver funnel and pulled it toward her, resting its lip against Maddy's arm so it could catch the blood as it rolled in thick crimson drops down her skin. As it dripped into the funnel, Fachtna swung it away and held it over the Morrighan's veiled face. Maddy rolled her sleeve back down and pressed it against her arm as they waited. Slowly a bulbous red drop appeared at the end of the funnel and swelled, before its own weight caused it to tumble down onto the black gauze that covered the Morrighan's mouth. Another appeared and then another, until seven drops had pattered onto the veil and sunk beneath its fragile fibers.

They all leaned over, holding their breath. Seconds ticked past. Still the Morrighan lay as still and lifeless as a statue.

Nero looked up into their faces. "What's supposed to happen now?" he asked.

Fachtna screamed with rage and struck at the funnel, slamming it off one of the bedposts. "WHY ISN'T IT WORKING?!" she roared.

"Maybe she needs a different type of blood," suggested Danny. "Maybe waking the Morrighan is the same as unlocking the mound."

Fachtna turned to look at Roisin.

"Oh no," said Roisin, backing away and turning to run. She screamed as Fachtna lunged at her and grabbed her wrist, dragging her back toward the bed.

"Let go of her!" yelled Danny, but Maddy stepped in front of him before he could do anything. Nero crouched and snarled, looking from Fachtna to Maddy, uncertain what he should do.

"It's still a good deal, Danny," she said.

"What are you saying?" said Danny. "You want me to stand and watch while Fachtna cuts her? You can't force her, Maddy!"

"You're right," said Maddy. She looked over her shoulder at Roisin. "Ro, you need to do this," she said gently. "You know you do."

"I'm sorry," said Roisin, tears spilling down her cheeks. "I'm such a coward."

"No, you're not," said Maddy. "You can do this."

Roisin squeezed her eyes shut, holding out her arm. Fachtna let go of her and began to roll her sleeve up while Roisin sobbed, snot bubbling from her nose. "I'll be quick, little chick," she said gently. "You'll hardly feel a thing." Roisin squealed as Fachtna's blade flashed down and she wept while the funnel was held against her arm and then over the Morrighan's face.

This time the effect was electric. The figure in the bed sat up and her wings flew out to the sides, stretching to their full length and sweeping them all off their feet. Her veil was sucked back against her face as she dragged air into her lungs, and as she reached out to a bedpost for support Maddy saw that the nails on her hands were curled into little black spirals too, just like those on her toes.

As her wings beat the air, sending up clouds of dust, the veiled face turned to look at Fachtna, who was crawling through the bones to prostrate herself at the Morrighan's feet, her forehead touching the ground, her wings folded tightly against her back and her arms outstretched.

"**Fachtna**," she said, in a voice that sounded like three people talking simultaneously—the high tones of a young girl, the deeper ones of a mother, and the cracked voice of an old lady. "**My captain**."

chapter thirteen

"My favorite has returned to me," said the Morrighan, bending down to cradle Fachtna's pointed face in her hands. "You were always so pretty, but war has made you beautiful."

"My queen," said Fachtna, looking up at the Morrighan. Maddy was horrified to see tears, actual tears, rolling down the faerie's mottled face. Maddy didn't even realize Fachtna could cry. "I have missed you."

"And yet you did not love me enough to stay," said the Morrighan. "You left when the rest of my court stayed to watch over me. You deserted your post and abased yourself by serving one who had only risen high by my hand."

Maddy looked around the dusty, rotten room, with its carpet of bones. *Yeah, because you'd be crazy to leave all this,* she thought.

Fachtna groveled with her face to the ground again. "Forgive me, my queen," she rasped. "I was weak. I craved the sunlight and the wind on my skin. I craved the excitement and the glory of battle and I longed for the taste of blood on my lips." She looked up at the Morrighan, who cocked her veiled head toward her. "But Tír na nÓg is in turmoil once more and I have returned to you, to fight again by your side."

"**Ah, but you do it for your own selfish reasons,**" said the Morrighan. Fachtna looked up at her, her eyes widening in confusion. "**I have been asleep, child, not dead. I still know what happens in my realm and I can still see into the heart of my former captain. Robe.**"

Fachtna sprang up and picked up a black velvet robe that had been lying at the foot of the bed. She held it out to the Morrighan, who slipped it over her naked body, her wings stretching out so they could slip through wide slits slashed through the back of the garment. It had a small, high collar and wide sleeves, and fell away from the Morrighan's shoulders in a straight line to her ankles. It was covered in silver embroidery depicting dragons much like the carved ones that guarded the door to this place. Little clouds of dust puffed into the air as she moved, but the Raven Queen continued to glow in the moonlight.

Fachtna was still standing behind her, smoothing the fabric over her neck and back when the Morrighan said, "**You come to me now, Fachtna, because you have grown greedy with your new queen. You no longer**

think of how you can serve, but rather what you can gain. And as your new mistress dooms herself with her madness, your hungry eyes are cast upon her crown. You have forgotten your place." Behind her Fachtna froze, her face a mask of despair. "**You are a good servant, Fachtna, but you would be a terrible monarch. Be content with what you have and look no further. I have already raised an outsider to a throne, and look at the harm she has done. I will let no other assume a Tuatha's place in this world.**"

Fachtna looked at Maddy, her eyes burning with anger. Maddy felt her heart sink. There would be no deal, no protection. And now the Morrighan was awake, Maddy could only hope the coming battle would go her way and they could all go home alive.

"**You have brought me a Hound,**" said the Morrighan, her veiled head swinging toward Maddy. Maddy felt Danny and Roisin tense beside her. "**How the smell of a hero's blood fills the room.**" The Morrighan continued, walking toward them, her spiraled toenails snapping off as she moved down the steps of the dais. She leaned down to Maddy, her wings spreading, casting a shadow over all four of them. Nero laid his ears back and cringed as the Morrighan's head drew closer. "**I do not know how to feel, having a young Hound in my hall. Do you know the trouble your kind has caused me? And yet I see the bonds that bind you. Why does Meabh want a Hound in her court? Why does she extend her protection over you?**"

Maddy swallowed as the Morrighan cocked her head to the left and to the right. After a couple of tense moments and an elbow in her side from Roisin she realized the faerie was looking for an answer.

"I . . . I don't know," she said. "She says she wants me to run for her."

The Morrighan leaned closer and brought her huge hand up to Maddy face, stroking her cheek with the pads of her fingers. **"But where does she want you to run to, little Hound? That is the right question."**

Maddy looked at her, her mind blank. Then a bright light flared through the windows and illuminated the hall as if it were day.

"Ah, now come the rest of my greedy kin," said the Morrighan. **"Fachtna, attend me."**

Fachtna crossed the room and hefted a heavy carved chair into her arms. She carried it to the foot of the dais and beat at its velvet seat with her hand to clean some of the dust from it. The Morrighan seated herself, her clawed hands resting on armrests shaped as a lion's paws, her back straight and proud. They waited, listening to the sounds of booted feet on the stairs outside. The heavy stone door swung open and Tuatha guards filed in, dressed in the green and silver livery of the Spring Court. They were helmeted and armed for war, every one with their hand on the hilt of a sword belted around their waist. Butterflies fluttered into the room as the light that radiated from the Spring King and Queen began to filter through the doorway. They flew and skipped in the miserable tomb, the jewel-colored wings bringing flashes of life to the shadows. Maddy drew in her breath as the light became stronger and then Queen Sorcha and King Nuada walked toward the Morrighan, Sorcha's hand resting on her husband's arm.

They were so beautiful. Sorcha's long blond hair almost reached the ground, straight and fine as water; it hung in glossy curtains around her face, kept back from her eyes with a gold circlet. Her eyes were a violet blue, her lips a warm cherry red, and butterflies flitted all around her, stroking her skin adoringly with their soft wings to leave streaks of glittering pollen on her face and neck. Her simple white dress was bound at the waist with a golden belt and embroidered with birds and animals. Nuada, her husband, could have been her twin, with his thick blond hair curling to his shoulders and his dark-blue eyes. They walked with their backs straight, their faces cold and proud. The glow of spring that radiated from their bodies brought color and fresh-ness back to the hall, showing what it had been like before the Morrighan lay down for her centuries-long sleep and it rotted all around her.

Maddy craned her neck to look up into Sorcha's beautiful face as she swept past, herself and her hus-band inhumanly tall and regal. But even though she loved to look at the Spring Queen, instinct still made her step back into the few shadows that still lingered in the hall. Danny, Roisin, and Nero crept after her. They had not forgotten how much Sorcha hated humans and the Hound most of all. Sorcha had wanted Maddy killed as soon as the Tuatha had found out she was the new Hound. She had been furious when she discovered Meabh had taken her into the Autumn Court.

Next came Meabh's Tuatha soldiers in their red and black livery. Maddy smiled to herself as she imagined the argument that must have taken place on those narrow stone steps over who should walk up them first. She was surprised that Meabh, a consummate politician, had lost. Perhaps her soldiers simply hadn't rowed fast enough?

Meabh's light was more subtle, a shifting flicker of candlelight that mingled with the scent of rain. Having lost two husbands in mysterious circumstances, she walked without a consort, only the Pooka, pressed close to her side as usual. The storm hags scuttled in her wake, trying not to step on the tangled red hair that dragged like a train on the ground. Her golden circlet was studded with rubies and she looked around the hall with an amused expression on her face. The soldiers from her court lined up on the opposite side of the hall to Sorcha's, Autumn Tuatha jostling Maddy, Danny, Roisin, and Nero deeper into the shadows. The three monarchs went to stand before the Morrighan and bowed deeply from the waist.

"The Spring Court rejoices to see you awake, Great Queen," said King Nuada. "The joy of your awakening ripples through Tír na nÓg and brings your subjects to your side to feast their eyes upon your countenance—"

The Morrighan gave a hiss of irritation and a twitch of her shoulders at the Spring King's elaborate speech. Nuada stuttered and trailed off into an embarrassed silence.

"We knew you would not desert us in our hour of need," said Sorcha simply.

"**Need?**" said the Morrighan. "**I find that a strange way to describe the situation, Sorcha. It seems that once again I have been awoken to sort out the petty squabbles of monarchs, monarchs who cannot be happy with the powers and the territories that I have gifted them.**"

"In our defense, Great Queen, this war has been forced upon us by one who is not a Tuatha—" said Sorcha.

"**And yet raised to a crown by me,**" interrupted the Morrighan. "**Are you daring to suggest that the coming war has been caused by me because I did something . . . foolish?**"

Sorcha's pale cheeks flushed. "I would never dare to suggest such a thing."

"**But yet, you think it?**" asked the Morrighan, an edge to her layered voice.

"No, my queen!" said Sorcha.

"I think what my dear sister is trying to say," said Meabh, her voice oozing honey, "is that the experiment of allowing an outsider to rise to high estate in our world in the interests of keeping balance has failed. Liadan has proved to be too unstable, too mentally and physically feeble, to carry the responsibilities of a

Tuatha crown. It is time to put an end to her reign and to consider anew the best way to keep peace among us all."

The Morrighan sat back in her chair. "**I agree. What do you think, my beautiful and clever witch queen, is the best way to do that?**"

"Bestow the Winter crown on a Tuatha, as it should have been all along," said Meabh. Sorcha and Nuada both gave a scornful bark of laughter, but the Morrighan silenced them by holding up one hand. Her face was still turned toward Meabh.

"**Do you have anyone in mind?**" she asked.

"I think that the crown would best come to Autumn," said Meabh. "I think I am the strongest of the monarchs and best able to lead two courts."

"It should go to my husband!" said Sorcha. "He could become King of Winter while I rule Spring and that way balance is restored."

Meabh laughed. "Please, Sorcha, do not pretend your husband has a mind of his own. Everyone knows he does exactly what you say and how tight his leash is. Giving the Winter crown to Nuada would be no better than giving it to you. And, frankly, it would be wasted on you."

"You dare to insult me . . ." began Nuada, his face going red with anger, but the Morrighan interrupted him as if he hadn't spoken. "**And why would it not be wasted on you, Meabh?**"

Meabh drew herself up to her full height, all seven feet. "Tír na nÓg must move on, it must evolve," she said. "Things have remained static for too long. We must be brave and reach out into new territories, and that will take a strong ruler if you are to return to your sleep. One ruler, with a single purpose, not swayed by the influence of a spouse."

"**Meabh, you have schemed for this for so long, your motives are transparent**," said the Morrighan. "**By new territories, you mean old ones, the mortal world. By evolve, you mean step back into the past. No Tuatha will return there to rule as long as I am High Queen. We made a pact with the mortal world when they drove us beneath the mounds—access to their nightmares and dreams for the nourishment of faeries and the maintenance of Tír na nÓg, in return for peace.**"

"With respect, my queen, the mortal world has changed—" said Meabh.

"**The treaty with the humans holds as long as I am High Queen,**" said the Morrighan. "**My purpose is to keep my people safe and this I have done for centuries. So unless you wish to challenge my right to … rule?**" The Morrighan let the question hang in the air. Sorcha and Nuada looked at Meabh and every soldier in the hall bristled as they waited for Meabh's response.

Meabh bowed from the waist. "Of course not, my queen. You have my allegiance, as always." The entire hall seemed to relax and let out a silent sigh of relief.

"**Then drop this foolish notion of invading the mortal world,**" said the Morrighan. "**Your throne in Connacht is gone, Meabh, and you cannot return to the past. So cut that Hound loose. I know you intended to use her against her own people, to dishearten the Sighted by seeing their own Hound come against them on the side of a Tuatha. So either let the Hound run home or kill her. She is neither use nor ornament to us.**"

Maddy shivered with fear as she watched Meabh bow again, with not a hint of protest on her lips. She would never have helped the Tuatha back into the mortal world, but now she and her cousins and poor Nero were alone and friendless in a hall with five hundred Tuatha.

"**Where is your sister?**" the Morrighan asked. "**Where is the Queen of Summer and her king? Do Niamh and Aengus Óg not long for Winter's crown? Even if they harbor no ambitions in their breast, why do they not come pay homage to their High Queen?**"

"We know not, my queen," said Sorcha, while Meabh remained silent.

The Morrighan gave a hiss of anger. "**Very well. We shall have a council of war and decide what is to be done about Liadan. I assume my brother, Cernunnos, finds himself obliged to lead her troops?**"

"He does," said Nuada.

The Morrighan shook her head. "**An ill-advised marriage. But he was so keen to settle all peacefully. Come.**"

And with that, the Morrighan stood and swept from the hall, the soldier Tuatha bowing to her as she passed, the other monarchs trailing in her wake. Maddy kept her eyes on them as they bowed, waiting to see if now would be a good time for them to slip away.

Then she felt a hand clamp over her mouth.

chapter fourteen

MADDY KICKED AND STRUGGLED AS AN ARM WRAPPED around her chest and lifted her off her feet. She found herself being dragged behind one of the rotting, dusty tapestries that concealed a narrow, claustrophobic stairwell, lit dimly by torches that smoked greasily. She heard a yammering shriek from Nero and then an ominous silence followed by more banging and scuffling. She was set down on the stairs, held by the neck of her jacket, and dragged along as if she were a kitten.

As her feet slipped and stumbled on the stairs, Maddy twisted to look over her shoulder and glared at the granite-faced Tuatha who had her tight in his grip. It was hard to see who was behind her as the stairwell turned in a tight spiral, but she caught a glimpse of Roisin's white, tear-streaked face before she was whisked around another bend.

"What are you doing?" she asked the Tuatha. "Where are you taking me?" But in answer he simply shook her so hard it made her teeth ache and she was convinced she felt her brain knock against the back of her eyes. Still the Tuatha dragged her without a sound, up and up and up, until she was so tired she seriously considered just letting her feet dangle and leaving the Tuatha to do all the work. There were no windows, nothing that could tell her where she was in the castle, just gray stone that wept with damp, even on a summer night. But as they carried on climbing, Maddy guessed they must be in the tall, narrow tower that emerged from the middle of the castle.

After what seemed like an eternity, the stairs finally stopped at the threshold of a small wooden door, arched and bound with bronze. The Tuatha knocked and Maddy heard a woman's voice telling them to come in.

The room had bare stone walls and flagstone floors. A small window punched through the four-foot walls gave a glimpse of the night sky beyond. There was no furniture, no tapestries, not a shred of cloth or color to soften the place. A woman stood looking out the window. She was another Tuatha, judging by her height, and she was dressed from head to foot in a pale-blue velvet cloak. As Maddy was dragged into the room she had a horrible feeling that she knew who she was looking at. But it was only when a yellow-and-white butterfly escaped the folds of velvet and came fluttering over to her that she knew. As Maddy was thrown to the floor the Tuatha turned and pushed the velvet hood back with long white hands laden with rings.

She could have been Sorcha's twin except her hair tumbled down in curls and her face had an open, innocent look, in stark contrast to Sorcha's stern intelligence. Like the Queen of Spring, the Summer Queen had her own retinue of butterflies that fluttered in the confines of her cloak, bathing in the golden light of summer that radiated from her body. In her simple blue dress she looked like an angel, albeit an angel who liked a lot of jewelry. Maddy had always thought she was a bubblehead—vain and self-obsessed. But there was a cunning look in her blue eyes that she had not seen before and it made Maddy's skin prickle with unease.

"Maddy, how good to see you again," Niamh cooed, her voice as sweet as the high notes of a violin. Danny and Roisin were dragged in behind her and shoved against the wall. "Tie those two up," Niamh commanded. "I don't want them interfering."

Another guard in Autumn livery walked in with Nero's still body in his arms.

"What happened to him?" asked Maddy.

"They knocked him out," said Danny as his arms were yanked behind his back and tied with rope. Roisin was weeping silently, her head bowed as she was trussed up like a Christmas turkey.

"Why would you hurt him?" Maddy asked Niamh.

The Summer Queen simply raised an eyebrow. "I am hardly going to risk a Tuatha being bitten by that cur, am I?" she said.

Light footsteps sounded on the stairs outside and Meabh walked into the room, her eyes sparkling with excitement and her cheeks flushed.

"I got away as soon as I could," she said to Niamh, "but we need to be quick. The final ingredient is on its way. Out of the room, all of you," she commanded the guards. "One of you must stand guard outside, but the rest are to report back to your captains."

"What are you doing?" asked Maddy.

Meabh walked up to her, smiling lazily. She cupped Maddy's chin gently in her hand and raised her face up so they were looking into each other's eyes.

"I'm going to unlock your true potential tonight, Maddy," she said. "You are going to get so many answers and then, just like I said you would, you're going to run for me."

"No, I won't," said Maddy. "I know what you are trying to do, Meabh. I'm not going to let you into my world and I am certainly not going to fight my own kind for you."

"That's the problem with Hounds," said Niamh, showing her little white teeth in a very unladylike yawn. "They always think they know their own minds." She considered this for a second. "I mean, they always think they should *have* their own minds."

"You're going to do exactly what I want, little Hound," said Meabh. "Do you know why? Because by the time

I am finished with you, what I want will be what you want."

"In what parallel universe is that going to happen?" asked Maddy, jerking her face out of Meabh's hand.

"Do you remember, once we talked about all that hatred and rage coiled up in that scrawny little form of yours?" purred Meabh. "You thought you had gotten rid of it. You thought you were a different person. But all you did was lie to yourself and call your hatred and rage something else—moral, righteous, words that felt good on your tongue and in your mind and let you rest easy. But I am going to let you look right into the dark heart of yourself tonight, Maddy, and when I do, you're going to see that these are not bad emotions. They don't make you a bad person. They are the best part of what you are, they are your strength, your salvation. And it's all there inside you, waiting to be unlocked."

"That's not who I am," said Maddy. "I made some mistakes last year. I didn't think clearly, but I paid for them—"

"No, you didn't," interrupted Niamh. "As I recall, someone else died because of your stupidity."

Stricken with guilt, Maddy felt the blood drain out of her face.

"Maddy, all your problems stem from the fact that you will not embrace what you are," said Meabh. "You struggle against your true nature and you struggle against the ones who would love you for it."

"No," said Maddy, shaking her head and blinking away tears. "You want me to become some hateful, twisted creature and I don't want to be that kind of person. I won't let you make me into someone like that."

"Liadan had the right idea when she lured you in here," said Meabh as she began to pace around Maddy. "She knew you were the key to unlock the mound on this side. She knew all that hatred and rage were powerful weapons that could punch through the barrier and let us loose. But she didn't know all the ingredients that were needed to make such a weapon. She didn't realize that what she also needed was the mist of dreams."

Maddy shuddered.

"All those twisted souls looking for comfort inside that mist, wandering around aimlessly, making part of Tír na nÓg uninhabitable for the rest of us," Meabh continued. "All that pent-up rage, that longing to return home. But they are sheep who need to follow someone. And they won't follow a Tuatha, they hate us so. Guess who they will run bleating after?"

"A Hound?" said Maddy in a tiny voice.

"A Hound!" said Meabh. "One of their own people, whose blood is like a siren's song. A Hound can lead them out of the Shadowlands, a whole army of split souls, and all that rage and hate and combined longing for the mortal realm on the other side of the mound will create a weapon strong enough to overcome the barrier that separates the worlds. And where your army goes, a Tuatha army will follow."

"I am never going to do that for you!" yelled Maddy. "Why would you think I would willingly sign up for an end-of-the-world plan like that?"

"I don't think any of us truly knows the extent of what you would do, Maddy," said Meabh, cocking her head toward the door at the sound of more booted footsteps ringing out on the stone and, beneath that, the sound of something heavy being dragged. "You're a Hound that has never been blooded. Once you kill, you'll be overcome with bloodlust and you will follow anyone who promises you battle and glory, like all the Hounds before you. You wanted to follow in Cú Chulainn's footsteps?" The door to the room flew open and two more Autumn soldiers entered, dragging someone between them. "Now you will get your chance."

"Ah, 'tis the faerie who would be queen," said Niamh in a mocking tone. "Looking a little bedraggled for royalty."

It was Fachtna.

The soldiers threw her facedown onto the floor. As she lifted herself onto her arms, Maddy could see her face was swollen and bruised and her white hair hung limp and sweaty across her face. One leg was soaked in blood, and when Fachtna tried to get up, she could only brace herself against one knee. They had hamstrung her.

Meabh bent over Fachtna and drew her sword, throwing it at Maddy's feet, while Niamh hissed at the soldiers to get out. Maddy looked at Meabh in confusion as the sword rang on the flagstones.

"A gift for you, little Hound," said Niamh.

"I don't understand," said Maddy, looking at Fachtna. The faerie looked up through her tangled mane of hair with angry red eyes.

"Now is your chance to kill Fachtna," said Meabh. "We knew it wouldn't be a fair contest, so we gave you a helping hand."

"A helping hand?" said Maddy. "She'll never walk again!" Niamh giggled. "She won't need to."

"The Morrighan will be angry that you've done this," said Maddy. "Fachtna's her favorite."

"The Morrighan isn't going to care," said Meabh. "Fachtna has proved herself twice a traitor—the Morrighan knows better than to trust such a creature as that. She has also coveted a Tuatha's rightful place and that is unforgivable." She curled her lip in contempt as she looked at the stricken faerie. "She is worthless to the Tuatha now."

"Killing her would be a mercy," agreed Niamh.

"I'm not doing it," said Maddy.

"She has tried to kill you," Niamh pointed out.

"Yeah but, to be fair, she hasn't tried that for ages," said Maddy.

Meabh stepped over to Maddy. "I told you once that you and Fachtna had much in common. Do you remember?" Maddy nodded. Meabh placed her cool fingers over Maddy's eyes, plunging her into darkness. "Then See."

Absolute black descended on her vision and Maddy felt her eyes straining in their sockets as they sought out a scrap of light. Her vision began to clear a little and dim shapes started to come into view. But she wasn't in that little room at the top of the tall tower anymore. She was in a small dark space . . . a car! She could see the dashboard glowing green, feel the engine rumbling through the seat. But everything was tilted to the side and, now that she could see a little more clearly, the glass on the windshield was cracked and blind.

No, she thought. *They wouldn't send me here!*

Cautiously she eased forward between the front seats, and a sob caught in her throat. There was her father, slumped sideways, his head resting against the window, cracks radiating in the glass around his skull. She knew this wasn't real, she knew she wasn't really here, on that freezing cold night in Donegal when her parents' car had skidded on ice and left the road, flipping over as it went. It was a like a movie that the faeries could play back to her, a movie that she felt she was in. But this *was* the past—her parents were gone and nothing that she did here was going to change that. She couldn't turn back time and have her life back to the way it was before, safe in London with her parents, surrounded by iron, blissfully unaware that such a thing as faeries existed outside storybooks.

Still, she reached out with a shaking hand and caught a little piece of her father's jacket between the tips of her fingers, a wail of anguish breaking through her clamped lips. Three years ago the younger Maddy would have shaken him, crying, "Wake up, Daddy, please wake up!" but now she knew there were no happy endings. Hot tears scorched her face and she felt as if she couldn't breathe through the hard lump lodged in her throat.

A groan from the passenger seat made her whip her head around. Her mother had lived for a few moments; Una had told her that. The little banshee had crept to her mother's side and held her hand as she looked into another world, before closing her eyes and slipping away as easily as falling asleep. Her mother's green eyes were looking straight at Maddy, but she didn't see her.

Maddy couldn't help it. "Mommy?" she asked in tiny voice.

The tinny screech of metal made her look up and she froze as she watched a long, white, tattooed hand drag a talon down the side of the car, one more scratch that wouldn't be noticed by the Guards in the ruined bodywork. Rage built up in her as she watched the tall white fairy, with her gray tattoos, her stiffened hair, and that distinctive damaged wing walk away from the car, a departing actor illuminated by the headlights until the deep night of the deserted country road swallowed her whole.

Maddy squeezed her eyes shut, and when she opened them again she was back in the tower, Fachtna's sword

in her hand. She could feel the weight of it making the
muscles of her arm tremble and she braced the point
beneath Fachtna's breast.

"Why did you do it?" she asked, her breath hot in her
mouth, heated by the lava of rage that bubbled in
her belly. She was dimly aware of Danny and Roisin
shouting but she couldn't hear their words over the
pounding of blood in her ears. "Tell me why."

Fachtna looked up at her and brushed her hair from
her eyes with a lazy gesture. "I was following orders."

"That's no excuse," said Maddy.

"Fine," said Fachtna. "It's my nature. As it is yours."

"I'm nothing like you!" said Maddy.

"Steel in our souls, little Hound," said Fachtna. "I
told you once—you do what you think is necessary,
and soon you stop being surprised at what you will do.
But let me give you one piece of advice." She reached
up the length of the sword with her long, mottled arm
and wrapped her fingers around Maddy's fist, leaning
into the point of the blade until blood bloomed. "Never,
ever, live on your knees." She smiled at Maddy, her full
lips covering the shark's teeth, and then she drove the
sword through her own chest.

chapter fifteen

MADDY SCREAMED AS FACHTNA'S WEIGHT FELL against her and her legs buckled as they both fell to the ground. She rolled Fachtna onto her back and crouched over her. She could hear Roisin screaming and cries of rage from Meabh and Niamh, but she ignored them all and leaned down, her tears splashing onto the war faerie's face.

"What have you done, Fachtna?" she sobbed.

"What was necessary," whispered the faerie, the breath fading from her lungs. "So you wouldn't have to." She smiled up at Maddy and gently laid a sword-callused hand against her cheek. "Tears for me? Who would have thought it, from the Feral Child! It wasn't that long ago we tried to kill each other."

"The good old days," said Maddy, smiling through her tears.

"You're a good girl," said Fachtna. The light faded in her red eyes, her mouth went slack as the last of her breath escaped and her hand fell away, the fingers limp. Maddy stared down at Fachtna, her anger draining away with her tears. The door burst open behind her and more people crowded into the room, but she ignored them all as she rocked over Fachtna's body.

Would she have killed her? Had she been angry enough to drive that blade through? She didn't want to be the person Meabh said she was, but for a moment she almost was. She couldn't trust herself. She looked down at her own body and felt sick. There was blood on her clothes—Fachtna's blood, on her hands, seeping into the lines of her skin, swirling through the whorls on her fingertips. She was dizzy and the room felt too hot and crowded. She staggered to her feet, the shouting voices all around clanging wordlessly in her ears. She shoved past them, her filthy hands batting aside silks and velvets to get to the door.

She gulped in the cold air of the stairwell and staggered down the steps, clinging to the rough stone walls for support. She pushed at the dusty cloth of the tapestry curtain and out into the hall, stumbling toward the dragon door and the steps that led down to the jetty. She was dimly aware of the handful of Tuatha soldiers lingering in the hall and their heads turning toward her as she crashed through the bones, but no one made a move to stop her.

Water, she kept thinking. *I have to wash my hands. I have to get the blood out.*

She shoved open the dragon door so hard she lost her footing on the stone steps. Her rubbery legs gave way beneath her and for one moment she thought she was going to tumble clumsily into the sea below her as she slid down the rail-less steps on her side, her feet flailing for purchase and her hands scrambling at the stone. After what seemed like an eternity, she stopped sliding and sank onto a step, taking great gulps of air into her lungs, shaking with relief, her clothes clinging to her with cold sweat.

She waited for her pounding heart to slow and for her breathing to return to normal, but her legs still felt boneless when she tried to stand. She sat back down with a hard bump, terrified she would fall again and not be so lucky this time. But the water was tantalizingly close so she went down the stairs on her bottom, like a toddler, shuffling from step to step, pushing off onto the one below with her hands.

The long, flat Tuatha boats bobbed on the water, oars up but with no anchorage that she could see. Like Meabh's walnut shell, they simply bobbed in place, waiting for their crews' return. Dark shapes flitted around them, humped backs that breached the quicksilver waves with a blast of breath and dived again with a slap of a tail.

Selkies. She had forgotten about them.

She heard a splash and the sound of water dripping at the end of the pier. A selkie female had hauled herself from the water in human form and was crouched, watching Maddy. Seawater streamed from her long brown hair and her eyes, a rich and velvety brown with no whites. Her nose was wide and flat in her face, the nostrils broad slits that could be closed against water. Her webbed hands were splayed in front of her, and when she spoke Maddy could see the flash of ivory fangs.

"So much blood, little Hound," she said in a gentle voice. "You are truly a lost soul. But we can give you another purpose."

"How?" said Maddy.

"Meabh has shown you a truth that she believes in," said the selkie, "but truth is a jewel of many faces. I can show you another face. You can have a choice, little one, and what we are is the choices that we make."

"I won't become what Meabh says I am?" asked Maddy, taking a tentative step toward the selkie.

"Not unless you choose it," said the selkie.

"And you can show me a different way?"

The selkie held out her arms. "Come, little one."

Maddy walked over to the selkie, slipped to her knees, and leaned into her embrace. The selkie wrapped muscled arms around her, leaned to the side, and pulled Maddy over the edge of the jetty and into the dark waters with hardly a splash.

chapter sixteen

ROISIN SCREAMED AS SHE WATCHED FACHTNA drive the sword through her own chest. She watched as Maddy rolled her over and talked to the dying faerie, praying that somehow everything would still be all right. Through the blur of tears she willed Fachtna to breathe, to pull the sword from her chest and sit up, laugh even, as if the whole thing had been a bad joke. She pressed against Danny and could feel him shaking. She should say something to him, anything, but she couldn't take her eyes off Fachtna. Meabh and Niamh, on the other hand, were half out of their minds with rage.

"What is wrong with her?" cried Niamh, pulling at her golden hair. "Why can she NEVER do what she is told?!"

"Fachtna!" spat Meabh. "She just had to ruin it all. She couldn't make her death useful!"

"You said this would work!" snarled Niamh, stalking over to Meabh, her fists clenched at her sides and her butterflies bashing into one another in confusion.

"Well, it would have, if the stupid creature had done what she was supposed to and butchered Fachtna like a pig," said Meabh.

The two queens were face to face now, their beautiful faces twisted with anger and fear. "You said that giving her a taste of killing would unleash her dark half," said Niamh, her voice lowered to a growl. "Instead she's weeping over that treacherous faerie like a baby. Does she even HAVE a dark side?"

"Of course she does," Meabh snapped back. "Do you think I would have spent all these years scheming to get her into this position, whispering in Liadan's ear so she would send Fachtna to kill her parents, working with *you*—" her voice dripped with contempt—"to get her back in here with that storm? Would I have worked so hard to make sure the wound to Liadan's pride would stay raw so she would bait the brat, if she didn't have that twisted side to her that could be fashioned into a weapon?"

"Well, at the risk of sounding obvious, *dear sister*," said Niamh, "you need to unlock that potential in the next five minutes. Just in case you haven't noticed, we have committed treachery in the castle of the Morrighan, so I need to get into the mortal world very soon.

Did the old fossil at least say who she was going to give the Winter crown to?"

"I have no idea what she is planning to do with it, but she isn't going to give it to Sorcha or myself, and I doubt you're next in line. She was aggrieved you were not there to pay her homage," said Meabh.

Niamh groaned and raked at her hair with her long fingers. "What are we going to *do*? We should be halfway to the mound now with a suitably unhinged Hound, not stuck in the Morrighan's stronghold trying to think of another plan!"

Roisin watched as Fachtna's hand fell away from Maddy's face and her fingers curled, still and lifeless. She let out a sob. She had always been terrified of Fachtna, but they had just lost the closest thing to a friend they had in here.

Meabh whirled at the sound of Roisin's sob, her green eyes lighting up with glee.

"Silly me, I almost forgot we had spares," she said, with a gloating smile. Roisin and Danny shrank back against the wall, wishing they could burrow through the stone as the witch queen walked across and towered over them.

"They're not Hounds," said Niamh. "They're no good to us at all."

"Maybe not," said Meabh, her eyes flicking from Danny's face to Roisin's and back again, her pink tongue licking at her lips, "but the Hound loves them. We simply need her to get pleasure from killing. If revenge will not motivate her, maybe saving a loved one will."

Niamh looked at Danny and Roisin for the first time, her face lighting up. "Ooooh, I like that plan," she said. "That could work!"

Meabh stooped and cupped Roisin's face in one hand, digging her nails into her soft cheeks. "What do you think, little rabbit?" she asked. "How far would your cousin go for you?"

"Leave her alone!" said Danny.

Niamh squealed like a young girl and clapped her hands. "He has fight in him," she said. "What a good start!"

The door to the room crashed open and bounced off the wall close to Roisin's head. She shrieked and cowered against Danny as the heavy wood vibrated under the impact. The Morrighan strode into the room, followed by a black-haired Tuatha and soldiers in Spring's livery. Her huge black wings quivered with rage as she faced Meabh and Niamh and spread them wide to cast her shadow over them like an angel. White-faced and silent, the two queens dropped to their knees and trembled.

"**Treachery,**" hissed the Morrighan. "**First from my favorite and now from two of my sister queens. How dare you! How DARE YOU!**" She turned to the dark-haired Tuatha. "**King Aengus, did you know what your wife was planning?**"

"No!" said Aengus Óg. "I swear it."

"Then it seems you cannot govern in harmony with your wife, or that you are so dull-witted that she can sneak around in your kingdom and plan such schemes with a rival court without your knowledge. Or perhaps you are just a liar?"

Aengus Óg went white and a muscle jumped in his jaw, but his voice was soft and polite when he answered. "I can assure you, my queen, that I am none of those things."

"And yet something is amiss," said the Morrighan, before turning back to the trembling queens. **"You were told, Meabh, that the treaty with the mortal world would hold as long as I am High Queen. Yet not only have you gone against my wishes, but I also discover that you have actually been grooming a Hound, of all the Sighted, to breach the barrier between the worlds. And to compound your treachery, you have involved a fellow queen. What do you have to say?"**

Roisin saw Maddy climb to her feet behind Meabh and Niamh. She turned, looked around the room and straight at Roisin, but Roisin could tell she couldn't really see anything. Nothing was in front of Maddy's eyes now but Fachtna's face. Her eyes were unfocused, wide with horror, her chest hitched with sobs and she began to gag. She staggered away from Fachtna's prone body, past Niamh and Meabh, colliding with the Morrighan, swatting her velvet gown away from her face before shoving through the guards. The Morrighan turned her veiled face to watch her go.

Go, Maddy, go! thought Roisin.

"She's getting away," hissed Niamh.

"And where will she go?" said the Morrighan. **"The only boats here are Tuatha and they will not move without a Tuatha hand on the tiller. Do not try to distract me. How have you become so greedy and dishonest while I slept? To try to breach my treaty, to reach your hands out for another's crown—"**

"It was not greed or dishonesty that motivated me, it was love for my court and my people," said Meabh, holding her head high, her green eyes flashing with anger and pride.

"Meabh, the selfless, nurturing queen, thinking only of others," said the Morrighan in mocking tones. **"Have I truly lived to see this day?"**

"It's true!" said Meabh. Everyone in the room stiffened to hear her raise her voice against the Morrighan, and the hands of Spring's soldiers went to the hilts of their swords. 'You are forcing us to live by a treaty made thousands of years ago. The mortal world has changed. They no longer remember us or the treaty. They don't know what the mounds are or where they lead to, and they don't care! When we were first driven beneath the mounds you talked of how we had gone too far with mortals. We had ruled too harshly, been too cruel in our day-to-day dealings with them, until dying free became better than living under our rule. And so they found the courage and the strength to rise up against us. We lost many Tuatha in that war and I know it grieved you. You said we had to learn our lessons and that to keep our people safe there could be no more contact between the worlds.

"But I have been watching them over the centuries and the mortals have grown more numerous, spreading over the world like a plague. It seems the more of them there are, the less they value the lives of their own kind. You talked about our cruelty—well, mortals treat each other in ways we would shudder even to think of. They kill by the thousands, millions even. They set their best and most brilliant minds to work inventing new weapons to slaughter with. People starve to death in the mortal world while their leaders spend money on weapons. Yet they cry out for peace. It will not be like it was before. Mortals will welcome strong leaders, a firm hand on the reins. They have lost their way and cannot live in peace on their own or look after their kind. They must be made to. Mortals will welcome slavery."

The Morrighan said nothing and continued to tilt her veiled face toward Meabh's. Roisin watched her in horror. *She's not actually listening to this?* she thought. *She CAN'T be listening to Meabh!*

But Meabh clearly thought she was, and the Autumn Queen began to talk faster while she had the Morrighan's attention.

"Think of your own people, my queen. Trapped together in this world we turn on one another, like rats trapped in a nest. Sooner or later we will kill one another, and everything you have tried to protect—our culture, our people—will be gone. Cast aside these crowns of seasons, these pathetic imitations of the power and territories that were once ours. Let us join together and crush the upstart elf. Then we will go forth into the mortal world and take back what is rightfully ours. This balance you have tried so hard to maintain is crumbling. You can give the Winter crown to none but a Tuatha, and Liadan cannot be left alive. This might be a disaster for Tír na nÓg, but it could be turned into an opportunity for the Tuatha. Tír na nÓg's time is over. This is a new dawn in our history and you will lead it."

Still the Morrighan said nothing.

Meabh leaned forward and lowered her voice. "Give me the Hound," she said, "and I can make this happen for you."

A little color began to return to Niamh's cheeks and she looked up slyly at the Morrighan through her hair.

There was a scuffle at the door and a soldier pushed his way into the room, dropping to one knee in front of the Morrighan, who swung her strange face in his direction.

"I beg your pardon, Great Queen, but a selkie has taken the Hound," said the Tuatha, trembling as he kept his eyes on the Morrighan's feet.

"WHAT?!" Meabh screamed in frustration. Niamh began to weep with anger, gnawing on her fingers.

"**How did this happen?**" asked the Morrighan.

"The Hound went out onto the jetty and a selkie was waiting for her," said the guard. "They spoke to each other and then she went with it into the water."

"And you LET HER?!" raged Niamh.

The Tuatha blushed. "We did not think to bar her way. There was nowhere she could go."

"Is she dead?" the Morrighan asked Meabh.

"No, we'd hear that awful banshee shrieking across two worlds if she was," said Meabh. "They always know."

"Well, it seems the Hound has solved our dilemma for us," said the Morrighan. "Aengus Óg, speak to your wife and get her under control. I want to know she is not scheming in my train as we go to war. Meabh, you will have your soldiers ready to march. We are going to unite the courts and overwhelm Liadan by sheer force of numbers."

"But the Hound is loose," said Meabh. "We have to get her back! We cannot simply let her wander Tír na nÓg."

"I do not care what the Hound does," said the Morrighan. "Let her run home. I have Liadan and the Winter Court to deal with, and it seems I must handle Autumn and Summer too."

"But you know that I am right," said Meabh. "There is merit in what I say. If we think on this and decide, as one, that to march on the mortal world is best for the Tuatha, then we need to have the Hound in our hands."

The Morrighan shook her head. "I will not split our forces to chase the Hound."

"But we don't need to," said Meabh, turning to look at Danny and Roisin. "She will come to us, if we dangle the right bait. Once we have the Hound again, we can dispose of the spares."

"Oh no!" said Danny, scrambling to back away as Meabh advanced on them, but Roisin stuck her chin out and addressed the Morrighan. "I can give you what you want!" she said.

Meabh stopped in her tracks, her mouth agape, and then she began to laugh. "What could you possibly offer?" she sneered. "You have nothing to negotiate with."

But the Morrighan was looking at her.

"That's not true," said Roisin. "I can think of a way you can keep the crown on Liadan's head while making sure she can't cause any more trouble. You can restore balance and still have the courts only as strong as one another. And you can honor the treaty."

"If you can achieve all this for me, what do you want in return?" asked the Morrighan.

"Me and my brother, we want to go home," said Roisin. "I want you to give us safe passage through Tír na nÓg and back to the mortal world. I want your solemn promise no faerie will ever come near me or my family again."

The Morrighan chuckled. **"Anything else you would like?"**

Roisin looked down at Nero, still unconscious by her feet. His mouth gaped slightly and his long tongue was pushed against his teeth.

"Yes. The wolves of Tír na nÓg are to come under your personal protection. No court will be allowed to hunt them, and they will be able to live in peace here for the rest of their lives."

"**You amuse me, little one, that you think you can negotiate with a High Queen,**" said the Morrighan. "**Tell me your plan, and, if I think it will work, I will agree to your terms. But if I suspect for one moment that you have been lying to me to buy a few hours of miserable life, or if your plan fails, I will kill you. Do you believe me?**"

Roisin looked at Fachtna's crumpled, bloody body, the way her white hair straggled on the ground. One guard was even standing on a chunk of her hair. Fachtna had been faerie kind and yet they had tortured her, condemned her to death, and now her body lay forgotten, as worthless as trash to them. Roisin was under no illusions what they would do to her and Danny if she gave them the excuse.

"I believe you," she said as a soldier cut the rope that bound her wrists. She rubbed at her arms to get the blood circulating again.

"**Speak on, little one,**" said the Morrighan. "**How are you going to give me my heart's desire?**"

"I need a couple of things to make this work," said Roisin.

"**Name them.**"

"I need an apple, some crystal or glass, and I need iron—a lot of it."

"**Where are we supposed to get you iron, girl? You know the stuff is poisonous to our kind. There's no more**

than a handful of it in Tír na nÓg, enough to find Hy Breasail and that's about all."

"I don't think that's true," said Roisin, looking straight at Meabh. The Autumn Queen looked startled for a moment and then it dawned on her what Roisin was thinking. She narrowed her eyes in warning, but Roisin talked on regardless, "I think Meabh has been stockpiling weapons to use against her own people."

chapter seventeen

BELOW ITS PLACID SURFACE, THE WATER WAS thick with seals. The selkie female kept her arms around Maddy as they dived, safe from prying Tuatha eyes. Maddy thought of Danny, Roisin, and Nero back in the castle and tried to struggle back to the surface, but the selkie had her locked in her embrace. Maddy's lungs began to burn as the air ran out and she thrashed around, terrified she would drown. When the selkie pinched her nose and held her head back, the last of her breath burst from her in bubbles and she was convinced the creature had tricked her and was now trying to kill her. But a dark shape swam up to her; a whiskered, fanged mouth was pressed to her own and stale air, secondhand air from another's lungs, was passed over. The pain in Maddy's lungs eased and she found all she had to do was signal with bubbles she needed more air and the whole process would be repeated.

At first her mind rebelled at not being able to control her body's breathing. Panic clawed and gibbered at the walls of her mind and Maddy twitched and squirmed in the selkie's embrace. But as the selkie swam on, stroking Maddy's head with one hand and hugging her close to her body for warmth, she began to relax. Seals rose to the surface and dived all around her, bringing back air from the nighttime world. The water almost rocked her to sleep. She could hear nothing but the deep, rolling voice of the sea and the cries of the seals as they called to one another. Her exhausted body gave up gratefully and her eyes began to close. She only dimly felt her head being tipped back and the press of mouths as she drifted deep into the blue velvet of sleep.

It was a blessing, as cool and soothing as balm on a painful burn. For the first time in almost two days Maddy was free of fear and pain. Her mind stopped whirling and she simply let someone else worry about everything. It wasn't her job, not anymore. It was a different world down here, one with its own rhythms and concerns. Tír na nÓg, with all its fear, might as well be on the surface of the moon for all Maddy cared. The mortal world, with all its pain, might as well be in another galaxy. Maddy's limbs went limp as she was towed along, the lights in her brain going out one by one.

So it was a shock when the voice of the sea started to get higher as they entered shallower waters. The world above the water grew brighter as a dawn sun rose and sent rays of light into the depths. The seals swirled around them, calling to each other with a series of grunts, clicks, and roars as the selkie began to climb toward the surface. They whirled around the selkie and Maddy, around and around and around, until the water boiled with their slipstream, bubbles of air clinging like pearls to their dark pelts.

It was almost painful to take a breath when their heads broke the surface. Maddy's lungs nearly burst with the strain as her body automatically dragged in as much of the crystal-clear air as it could. She could feel her sinuses crackling and the corners of her mouth tingled with pain as the oxygen flooded her body. A seal shot up from the depths and breached the surface next to her, flopping onto its back and yawning into the light. It rolled over and swam to Maddy, nudging and butting her with its round head.

"Get on his back," said the selkie. "We still have a long way to go."

Gingerly Maddy stretched out onto her belly as the seal dived beneath her and then slid his body under hers. She wrapped her legs around his torpedo form, but there was nothing to hold on to and the seal's pelt was smooth and slippery. As the selkie began to swim away with powerful strokes of her arms, Maddy laid her hand against the seal's neck and prayed she would not fall off.

It was awkward. Even though Maddy gripped as hard as she dared with her legs, she still found herself slipping backward into the water. The seal was constantly having to stop and flip her forward with a flick of his tail. She was sure she was getting on his nerves and at one stage she even mumbled a "sorry," but he gave no sign that he had heard. As they powered along, more seals rising and diving in the water around them as they followed, Maddy lifted her head into the summer sea breeze and tasted the salt drying on her lips. She felt clean and fresh, and when she closed her eyes against the sun's rays, her lids glowed carmine red.

Eventually a gray smudge appeared on the horizon, growing clearer the longer they swam. It was a barren and rocky shoreline, deprived of the smallest scrap of vegetation to soften its jagged edges. There was no sign of life, no animals moved, there was not even a single bird to puncture the sky above it.

The water became shallower until Maddy was able to climb from the seal's back and wade through the waves after the selkie, who was striding on ahead, her muscular thighs slicing effortlessly through the water. Maddy was out of breath by the time she caught up with her.

"We're in the Shadowlands, aren't we?" she asked the selkie.

"We are," the selkie replied, her eyes scanning the landscape around them.

Maddy swallowed against the knot of fear that twisted in her stomach. The only person she could remotely call a friend here was Finn mac Cumhaill, an ancient mortal hero. He brooded with his soldiers, the

Fianna, in the heart of the Shadowlands, where even faeries feared to tread.

She gasped and her legs went wobbly as the force of the revelation hit her. Of course! Finn mac Cumhaill was literally a living legend. As his story was kept alive in the mortal world, so was he kept alive in Tír na nÓg. She had no idea if he was a man, a ghost, or a story made flesh, but he had enough strength to keep himself out of the Coranied's cauldrons. Enough strength to make himself a force to be reckoned with. He and his men had made the Shadowlands their territory. He brooded in its depths, waiting for the return of his wife, a Tuatha who had been bewitched and turned into a white doe. If she was looking for an army, it was right here.

"Mac Cumhaill!" she cried, and the selkie turned to her and smiled. "He's the answer, isn't he? The other choice."

"He could be, if you can persuade him to act," she said.

"Oh," said Maddy, her sudden surge of hope escaping her as fast as air from a burst balloon. She had forgotten how mac Cumhaill had turned his back on the mortal world, how little he cared about what happened to it and all the people who kept his name alive. He hated the Tuatha, and both worlds could burn for all he cared. This could be tricky.

"Don't worry, little one," said the Selkie. "I am sure if anyone can persuade Finn mac Cumhaill to take up arms again, you can. But first there are others you must win to your side."

"Who?" asked Maddy.

"Them," said the selkie, raising her arm and pointing at the yellowish mist that was billowing toward them, the ground disappearing beneath its belly as it came. The mist of dreams.

The selkie turned and began to walk back to the water and to the seals that waited for her.

Maddy caught her arm as she went past. "It won't let me through," she said. "It's full of . . . things. They hate me."

"They are not things, child—they are your own kind, and you do not need to be afraid," said the selkie. "They have a longing for something that I think you know you cannot give. You must talk to them."

"And say what?"

The selkie smiled. "Do you now know what the Hound knows?"

"The Hounds only knew things other Sighted didn't because they were the only ones to walk in both worlds, weren't they?" said Maddy. The selkie nodded. "Then yes, I think I do."

"Then speak the truth to them," said the selkie. "They will recognize it. They are still human."

"Why did you help me?" Maddy asked.

"You're meant to be the doom of Tír na nÓg," said the selkie, "but that does not have to be. I think you can make better choices."

"What about my cousins and Nero?" said Maddy. "The Morrighan still has them."

"They will be safe from harm until this battle is over," said the selkie. "The Morrighan is not a gambler, and she will not throw away any advantage she might have. Your friends are safe for now. If you want to help them, then stay here and do the needful. Do not shirk from your path."

The selkie gently untangled herself from Maddy's grip and walked into the water, where a seal was holding a silver pelt in its mouth. Maddy watched as she bent and took the pelt, throwing it around her shoulders like a cloak. Her human body melted, the shoulders sloping and disappearing, the long brown hair receding, until it was a seal that disappeared beneath the waves.

Maddy turned away from the sea and took a deep breath. She walked toward the mist as it advanced and stepped inside it. She flinched as it rolled over her and the Shadowlands vanished.

The mist obscured everything. If Maddy lifted her hand in front of her face right now, she would not be able to see it. She looked down and realized she couldn't even see her legs. As the mist oozed she wiggled her toes to assure herself her feet were still attached. She fought down panic as voices began to whisper around her, angry voices, voices choked with tears, pleading voices—the amount of misery that swirled around her was overwhelming. Tears began to roll down her face and she clenched her hands into fists at her sides to stop herself from clapping them over her ears.

"Stop," she said. "STOP!"

The mist went quiet. The voices stilled and the mist rolled and heaved around her in silent greasy coils.

"I know what you want," said Maddy.

Part of the mist seemed to condense and darken in front of her. A human shape quickly grew an outline and stepped toward her. Features formed on the face, color began to seep into the body, until a six-year-old girl stood in front of her. Her shoulder-length black-brown hair was tied up in two braids, finished with a red ribbon. There was a smattering of freckles across her cheeks, and her face was broad with a snub nose. Maddy recognized her as the split soul who had attacked her the last time she was in the Shadowlands.

"Home," said the girl. "Take us home."

"I can't," said Maddy.

The girl looked at her with hatred and then her face began to crumple and she shrieked, a noise that went straight through Maddy's head and almost dropped her to her knees.

"Stop it!" said Maddy, her hands over her ears. "STOP IT!"

The girl closed her mouth and stood there glaring at Maddy. Maddy took her hands away from her ears, panting with stress.

"You can't go back," said Maddy. "You have all been in here for so long that the people you were separated from have died. You can't go home because it doesn't exist anymore!"

The voices in the mist began to wail while the creepy little girl carried on staring.

"But you don't have to wander in here, lost," said Maddy. "You still have a purpose, a function. You can do something that will make you feel human again, even if you can never again connect with the soul you were torn from."

The mist went quiet. Maddy looked at the little girl. "We're listening," she said.

Maddy took a deep breath and continued. "All this time you have been here, you have felt lost, weak, longing for a way back into the mortal world. But while you cannot go back to the world above, you are not weak. The Tuatha do not walk the Shadowlands because of you. You are pure essences of human emotion, pure pain that was formed when you were splintered apart from your soul, and the Tuatha are terrified of that. They might feed on human emotion, but have you ever wondered why they do not come after you, why the Morrighan does not use you to keep this place alive, why she still depends on the Coranied? You overwhelm them. Now Meabh would use your strength to break into the mortal world and to destroy everything that you ever loved, to lay waste to everything that makes us human. You can stop her."

"How?" said the girl.

"Meabh wants to fashion you into a weapon, with me at your head," said Maddy. "But I think you are numerous enough and strong enough to block the mound as well as open it. You can shore up the defenses of the barrier and become an army that would block the Tuatha at every turn. You cannot go home, but you can protect it. You could stop the faeries getting through even at Halloween and make sure that every child in Blarney sleeps safe in their bed. There is honor in living like that, rather than skulking in the Shadowlands, waiting for a Hound to lead you out."

Still the mist was silent. Still the creepy little girl kept glaring at Maddy as if she was dreaming of punching her face in.

Maddy sighed. "Whatever you decide, I need to get to Finn mac Cumhaill," she said. "Will you let me pass?"

The girl darkened and faded back into the mist. It swirled for a few moments and then began to pull itself apart, creating a path in front of Maddy's feet.

"Thank you," she said.

chapter eighteen

THE MORRIGHAN HAD TO RESTRAIN NIAMH FROM clawing at Meabh's face in her rage.

"You've been hoarding iron?!" Niamh screamed. "Why would you do that, except to use it against your own? How could you stoop so low?"

As she struggled to get past the Morrighan, her husband, Aengus Óg, was forced to step forward and clasp Niamh in his arms, pulling her away before she caused the High Queen offense.

"This won't be forgotten, Meabh," she spat. "When we have dealt with Liadan, it will be your turn!"

"Perhaps in the future you will be careful who you throw your lot in with when you decide to turn traitor," said the Morrighan, while Meabh stood silent and white-faced, her hands clenched at her sides. For once the witch queen was silent—she did not even try to deny Roisin's accusation. "**Do not forget what you have done today. Indeed, when Liadan is put down it will not just be Meabh who will be judged. I will have to look long and hard at your fitness to rule and your ability to wield power responsibly.**"

"I did what I thought was best for us all, even you, Great Queen," pleaded Niamh. "I had to take action—you could not be woken."

"**A child's excuse**," said the Morrighan. "**Perhaps it is your husband, who seems to be innocent in all this, and your husband alone, who can be trusted to rule the Summer Court.**"

Niamh gasped as Aengus Óg let go of her and stepped back, putting distance between the two of them. "How could you?" said Niamh, her cornflower-blue eyes welling with tears.

Aengus Óg shrugged. "We must be practical," he said. "We do not have just ourselves to think about. If I did not have an entire court depending on me, I would stay by your side out of love for you and defend you to the death—you know I would. But alas, a king has other considerations."

"Traitor!" Niamh hissed, her beautiful face contorted with rage, her tears forgotten.

"**Now you know how it feels**," said the Morrighan. She gave a whistle and Roisin could hear the beating of wings. A flock of ravens blackened the morning sun outside the solitary window, plunging the tower room into darkness. One peeled away from the flock and landed on the windowsill, its claws scratching at the stone as it turned its head this way and that, fixing the occupants with its beady black eyes. The Morrighan held out her arm.

"**Come to me, my dear**," she said. The raven gave a screech, spread its wings, and glided over to land on the Morrighan's arm, its black claws digging into her velvet robe. The Morrighan gently stroked the shiny feathers of its head. The bird dipped its head under her touch and half closed its eyes as it muttered with contentment. When the Morrighan stopped petting it, it stood up straighter on her arm, shook its head, opened its beak and very clearly croaked the word "Mistress."

Startled, Roisin looked at Danny, who looked just as surprised as she did. "**Ah, the memory of me has been handed down to you, little one**," said the Morrighan, cooing with delight. "**Your ancestors served me before I went to my great sleep.**" She turned to Roisin. "**Do you have paper?**"

"I think I do," said Danny. He shrugged off his knapsack and rummaged in it, pulling out a notebook and pen.

"**Hand it to Meabh**," said the Morrighan.

Danny shuffled forward, trying to keep his eyes averted from Meabh's angry eyes, and handed her the paper and pen while pretending to be fascinated by his own feet.

"You are to write instructions, Meabh, and this little one will carry them for us," said the Morrighan, stroking the raven's feathers.

"What would you have me write, Great Queen?" asked Meabh through stiff lips.

"You will tell your court to bring the iron out of hiding," said the Morrighan. "Tell them to meet us where the river flows into the Great Forest. Tell your artisans to bring all the crystal and glass that you have also. What do you need them to do with it, clever girl?" This last question was directed at Roisin.

"They need to start building a casket from the crystal and glass and bind it all around with iron so there is no escape," said Roisin. "Make it pretty, fit for a queen."

"You have written it all down, Meabh?"

"I have, my queen."

Meabh rolled the paper up into a tiny scroll and handed it to the Morrighan, who placed it in the raven's gaping beak. "Fly to Meabh's castle, little one, and find her captain." She threw up her arm and the raven flew for the window, disappearing into the brilliant blue of the summer sky.

"Now to deal with Liadan once and for all," said the Morrighan. "I must find the monarchs of Spring—they must be wondering at my manners, leaving them sitting in a room on their own. They will be delighted when they hear how many thrones may soon be vacant." As she swept out of the room she called over her shoulder,

"Wake that wolf up, unless one of you wants to carry him."

⤳

Danny and Roisin were finally left alone at the back of one of the Tuatha boats as they journeyed in a flotilla back to the devastated forest. Poor Fachtna's body had been left on the floor of the tower room. Roisin couldn't bear to leave her like that, like a piece of litter someone had thrown on the floor, so she had slipped off her hoodie and covered Fachtna's face with it, folding the faerie's hands over her wounded chest.

They huddled in the back of the boat, Nero at their feet nursing a sore head, while a single soldier kept a wary eye on them. Danny asked Roisin what the plan was.

"It's a bit more of a hunch than an actual plan," said Roisin. "But I think it will work."

"You're joking," said Danny. "Please, *please*, tell me it's a plan, seeing as all our lives seem to be depending on it."

"Look, all I know is that Liadan loves her stories; she thinks she's very clever playing them out," said Roisin. "Do you remember when we first came here and she set the wolves on us, playing out Little Red Riding Hood?"

"Yeah, I remember," said Danny, glaring at Nero. "I think I still have the scars."

"I apologized for that, didn't I?" said Nero.

"We influence this place," said Roisin. "I've done it three times now. It's built on human imagination and it responds to it—that's the way the magic in here works. So if my imagination is strong enough, I think I can trap Liadan in a story."

"That's what we are depending on?" said Danny. "You having a *really* vivid imagination? No offense, but I don't have total confidence in this plan."

"It's kept us alive so far, and it's the only chance we have of rescuing Fenris," snapped Roisin. "So unless either one of you has a better idea . . . ?" She looked between the pair of them. "No? Thought not, so shut your mouths then."

They sat in silence as they left the sea and entered the mouth of the river.

"What about Maddy?" asked Nero. "How are we going to get her out?"

"I don't know," said Roisin miserably. "We don't even know where she is."

"At least we know she is still alive," said Danny.

"For now," said Nero.

A shout went up from the boats at the front of the flotilla and Roisin craned her head to see what the excitement was about. She could feel shimmering waves of heat and the smell of woodsmoke drifting downstream toward her. For a horrible moment, she thought the forest was on fire again. But as the oars pulled them through the water and she could see the bank ahead more clearly, she realized that the Autumn Tuatha had built a massive temporary forge. Now she could clearly hear the sound of hammers striking iron and as the boats pulled close to the river bank she could see the Tuatha craftsmen hard at work, stripped to the waist in the searing heat. They wore huge gloves that stretched almost to their armpits to protect them from the poisonous iron.

As their boat drew alongside the bank, a Tuatha helped Roisin and Danny out and took them straight to the Morrighan. The Raven Queen had changed her clothes before they had left her isolated castle and now she stood clad head to foot in silver armor and black leather, her chasing silver dragons embroidered onto every surface, her face still veiled. She pointed to the pieces of casket that littered the grass.

"Is this what you had in mind, little one?" she asked.

Roisin quickly scanned the pieces. "Will it hold together, if it's being built in such a short space of time?"

"It will hold," said the Morrighan. "I have the final piece you asked for."

She reached inside her black cloak and held out a big, shiny red apple.

"Oh, that's not for me," said Roisin. "That's for you."

"For me?" said the Morrighan, her voice loaded with suspicion. "What kind of trickery is this?"

Roisin took a deep breath. "I need to tell you a story..."

chapter nineteen

THE MIST LED MADDY, STUMBLING AND SLITH-
ering on rocky, barren ground, to the gates of the forbidding castle. Rough-hewn and unadorned, it was
very like the Blarney Castle. It had the privilege of
being inhabited and it stood square and firm, unlike
Blarney Castle, with its crumbling teeth for battlements and its rotten interior where whole walls had
fallen away.

There were guards, mac Cumhaill's Fianna, on the
walls, their upper faces hidden by helms, long spears in
their hands. They wore blue plaid with leather breeches
and their arms and necks were ringed with bronze. One
of them leaned over to call down to her.

"Is that you back again, Hound?"

"It is," said Maddy. "I need another favor."

"Is that right?" said the guard. "The last favor you asked of Finn mac Cumhaill got nearly half of us killed by lightning strikes and angry trees."

"He got his dog back in the end, didn't he? But you'll love this one," said Maddy. "This time you get a chance to be impaled on the pointy end of a sword in battle. Against Tuatha."

The guard thought about it for a bit. "We heard the Tuatha were on the move. Is it true the Morrighan is awake?"

"It is."

"And is it true you were the one who woke her?"

"It is," said Maddy, crossing her fingers behind her back against the lie. The Fianna wouldn't be impressed by a rambling explanation of who did what.

The guard gave a low whistle of admiration and his comrades on the wall laughed, their teeth flashing white in bearded faces. "You picked a proper fight this time, Hound," he said. "Fair play to you. That's worthy of Cú Chulainn himself."

"So are you going to let me in so I can talk to Finn mac Cumhaill?"

"What, so you can drag us all into a battle that will result in certain death? I don't think so."

"Go on, you know you'll enjoy yourselves."

The Fianna roared with laughter on the battlements. "I'll say one thing for you, Hound—you have a fine tongue in your head," said the guard as he signaled for the gate to be opened. "Mind you don't cut yourself with it."

Maddy squared her shoulders and walked into the stronghold of Finn mac Cumhaill and the Fianna. They were the last mortals left who would ever stand up to the Tuatha. The Sighted adults in Blarney were too frightened, too cowed from all the years they had spent hiding away on Halloween night and then cleaning up the mess afterward. Finn mac Cumhaill had been the greatest hero Ireland had ever known. True, mac Cumhaill preferred to brood in his fortress rather than fight. But Maddy knew she just had to make him angry enough and then steer him in Meabh's direction.

When she walked through the heavy wooden gates into the courtyard of the fortress her spirits lifted. This might be easier than she thought.

The last time she had been here it had been like the castle of the dead. Mac Cumhaill's longing for his lost wife, his lethargy, his rejection of everything outside of his own misery had infected the place like a cancer. Not even noise had been allowed. When she had last walked through the Fianna stronghold, her footsteps had hit the packed earth with a dull noise that had faded instantly. The Fianna themselves had been dull-eyed and listless, men whose world had passed them by, marooned in time.

But now the Fianna gathered around her, laughing, slapping her on the back so hard that she was almost sent sprawling face down in the dirt as they crowded close. There was color in their faces again and their eyes sparkled with life.

"You all look . . . um, you're looking . . ." Maddy desperately groped for the right word, one that wouldn't offend the notoriously touchy warriors.

"Alive?" said one.

"Like real men again?" said another.

"Well, yeah," said Maddy. "What happened?"

"I think we needed to be reminded of who we were and get a taste of it again, even if it was only for a little while," said the guard who had ordered the gates open. "It felt good to ride in the woods again, to be on the track of a foe . . ."

". . . to be half killed by lightning strikes and angry trees?" said Maddy, remembering his words on the gate.

The Fianna roared with laughter again. It made Maddy a bit twitchy, they had changed so much.

"That too," he said. "There is nothing like the risk of death to remind you how good it is to be alive. When you come through on the other side, everything feels better, louder, sweeter, saltier."

"Right," said Maddy. "And how is mac Cumhaill?" she asked as the guard swung the wooden double doors to Finn mac Cumhaill's hall wide for her.

The guard lowered his voice. "He is better," he said. "Like us, he remembered what it was like to be really alive and not have your spirit trapped between the pages of a book. He came back to himself a little bit. But he still grieves. His grief has always kept him bound." The guard shook his head. "I have heard you have a honeyed tongue, little Hound, but you will have trouble bringing mac Cumhaill around to your way of thinking. He is still a High King and will only do what suits himself."

"I have to try," said Maddy. "You haven't heard what Meabh has planned."

She was about to walk through the doors when the guard stopped her with a hand on her shoulder. "If it all gets too much for you, little Hound, there is a place here for you among our ranks. It's a sore responsibility to set on the shoulders of one so young and you have our respect."

Maddy was shocked. She had always assumed the Fianna thought she was trouble. A warm feeling spread in her belly and she could have hugged the somber-faced guard.

"Thank you," she said. "Really, I mean that."

The life in the courtyard had seeped into the Fianna's great hall as well. A soft light filtered through the mist of dreams, bathing the shields and swords hung on the walls. Brightly colored banners were draped in soft folds around the hall and the floor was strewn with green rushes that gave off a sweet scent as Maddy walked on them. Cleanly scrubbed long benches spanned the width of the hall and the men who sat at them were laughing, talking, mending clothes, cleaning weaponry. All of them looked bright and alive.

But Finn mac Cumhaill still brooded. Although some of the color had come back into his face, he still sat on his dais, silent and unsmiling on his tall wooden throne that was draped in animal furs. He wore the same blue plaid as his men, his dark curling hair tumbling around his shoulders. Bran, his faithful wolfhound, was in her customary place by his knee. He no longer looked exhausted, but his grief was etched plain upon his face and his weeping women still sat at the foot of his throne. There were three of them, all with tears streaming down their faces. Their cheeks were marked with grooves where the water had worn a path, while the front of their dresses and their laps were dark and marbled from the salt. Mac Cumhaill would not weep for his wife, so he used the magic of Tír na nÓg to make these women weep for him, day and night, even when they slept, for the whole of their long existence in this place.

"Welcome, little Hound," said Finn mac Cumhaill. "I see you come to grace my hall again."

"I do, lord, but also to ask for aid," said Maddy.

Finn nodded. "It was always thus with Hounds. They always came to me with their hands outstretched."

"But they did not do it for themselves, lord, but for others," said Maddy.

"Does it matter? The point is they asked and always took. It made me grow weary," said Finn.

Maddy looked at the weeping women, condemned to be weighed down by another's grief for the rest of their lives. "You did it once yourself, lord, until you forgot who you are," she said, her eyes sparking with anger.

Finn glared at her. "You have big teeth for a little Hound, but tread carefully—pups can be drowned."

"Is that a threat?" said Maddy. "Because if it is, please, go ahead, let's just get it over with." She flopped to the floor and crossed her legs, bracing her elbow against her knee so she had something to rest her head on.

"I haven't slept for days, as usual, I smell, as usual, and this time the problems are bigger and I am completely on my own," said Maddy. Her voice cracked with unshed tears but she didn't care. It was all too much. She started crying, noisily and snottily, like a toddler. She knew she looked ridiculous and was probably ruining her reputation among the Fianna as the hard-nosed, brave Hound. "You're still as crazy as you were the last time I was here and I can't be bothered wasting hours persuading you to do what you *know* is the right thing to do. What's the point? Even if I end up saving the world again, there'll just be another problem tomorrow. I mean, if you, with your big army, can't be bothered to get off your great backside to help out your own people anymore, why the hell am I bothering?" Maddy hiccupped and wiped at her wet face with her sleeve.

Finn got up and slowly walked down the steps of his dais and over to Maddy, his feet soft in the rushes. He crouched down to look into her face and said, "What do you mean, that I am crazy?"

"Seriously?" said Maddy. "LOOK at them!" She pointed at the weeping women. "Who does that to someone else? So you miss your wife. OK, we get it, but you are actually forcing other people to grieve for her alongside you, and not just for a little while—oh no!

Those poor women have been grieving for centuries. Do you not think they might have something else they would like to be doing?"

"Like what?" asked Finn.

"ANYTHING!" Maddy screamed.

Finn looked over his shoulder at the women. "That is the way you are, Maddy. That's why everything around here is so attracted to you; it's not just the fact that you are the Hound. All that grief and rage, it's powerful stuff in a place like Tír na nÓg. You know that, you've known it for nearly two years now. You cry out that all you want is a normal life and still you hang on to this. You're no better than me."

"Oh no!" said Maddy. "See, that was the old me. I'm not going back to being like that, not if I get out of here alive. I love my parents so much, but if grieving for them every day and hanging on to the past means that I end up like you . . . no way. Life is for living, and if grieving too long turns you into the walking dead then I am going to start enjoying what I've got." Maddy cried harder. "Would your wife have wanted you to live like this? Would she? I know my parents wouldn't have wanted this much pain for me. And if you keep picking at the scab, the way you do with those poor women, the pain never gets any better."

Finn sat back on his heels and looked at her. Maddy stopped crying for a moment and looked at him hopefully, but his expression was unreadable.

"So what do you need to do?" he asked.

"I need to get out of here, in one piece, and pick up my two cousins on the way," said Maddy, sniffing back snot in a loud snort that would have her granny reaching for a hanky.

"And what do you need to do that?"

"I need big hairy men with big sharp swords, who can slow the Tuatha down for long enough so I can use the mist of dreams to lock the mound. Know anyone who's got some of them?" she asked.

Finn chuckled. "Lock the mound, eh?" he said. He looked at her with admiration. "That's a big task. Not even Cú Chulainn ever tried to do that. So what do you need us to do?"

Maddy looked up at him in shock while he roared with laughter, the men in the hall joining in. "I admit it, little Hound, your honeyed words have won me over. Who could resist such charm, such oratory?"

Maddy gaped at him. "You were going to help me all along? Then why didn't you say something?"

"Because it was amusing to watch you rage and let your tongue loose," said Finn. "We have little other entertainment here." He looked back over his shoulder at the weeping women, who gazed back, their seeping eyes hopeful. He frowned. "But you are right. Perhaps it is time to find a more fitting tribute to my wife. One that does not cause another person sorrow."

He stood up and held a hand out to Maddy, pulling her to her feet. "So I ask again, little Hound, what do you need the Fianna to do for you?"

"It's not much," said Maddy. "I need a distraction, something that will keep the Tuatha busy long enough for me to get to the mound on my own. I also need my cousins and two wolves to be rescued."

"Is that all?" said Finn. "You heard her, men! Get those weapons down from the wall, saddle up your horses, and unfurl your banners. The Fianna are riding again!" The men cheered and the hall burst into activity as they rushed to and fro, dogs jumping up and barking with excitement.

"So," said Finn, as the din of organized chaos crashed around them, "this distraction—do you have something in mind?"

"Funnily enough, this time I do have a plan," said Maddy.

chapter twenty

ROISIN CRINGED AS THE TUATHA ARMY CRASHED its way through the burned forest. Their giant white horses brushed against fragile trees, crumbling scorched bark in their wake. Their huge hoofs thudded down, sending up clouds of thick black soot. She could only imagine what the forest must be feeling as the army rode through on its way to the White Tower. *It must be like nails scraping over an open wound,* she thought.

The Morrighan was taking no chances that her prisoners would escape. Danny and Roisin had been lifted up onto the Tuatha horses and their mounts plodded obediently next to hers. Like their boats, Tuatha horses only did what the Tuatha willed. Roisin and Danny could have been expert riders, but nothing they could do would persuade these giant beasts to disobey the orders given to them by Tuatha. The Morrighan had not seemed to be too bothered about the possibility of Nero slipping away into the forest—at least she had made no attempt to restrain him. The gray wolf loped beside them, careful where he put his paws on the sharp carbon of the forest floor. Roisin knew he was desperate to get to Fenris and so far they had been making good time. The forest around them was silent and there was no sign of Liadan's soldiers.

The monarchs were also kept close, much to the disgust of Sorcha and Nuada, who insisted that they alone, of all the courts, were the only ones who remained loyal to the High Queen's rule. But the Morrighan was not convinced. Spring, Summer, and Autumn were all forced to ride with her and her human prisoners. Their combined troops spread out behind them, each under the command of a trusted captain. Everyone was sullen and unhappy and the monarchs rode in an angry silence.

Danny clung to his saddle, looking slightly green around the gills. He wasn't comfortable on horseback—the rocking movement always made him slightly seasick. Roisin couldn't make herself heard over the thundering of the hoofs and jingle of tack but she smiled at him and mouthed, *Are you OK?* He gave her a weak smile back and a thumbs up. Behind them, the casket had been wrapped in a rough brown cloth and placed on a cart and was being dragged by two mounted Tuatha.

A shout rippled along the front ranks and the Morrighan pulled her horse to a halt as a scout galloped along the line. He reined in before her, his horse's white coat gunmetal gray with sweat and ash, its chest foamy with saliva.

"**What news?**" said the Morrighan.

"There is no sign of any enemy, Great Queen, not even scouts," he said.

"**How far have you ranged?**" she asked.

"Twenty-five miles in all directions, Majesty," said the scout. "We are the only living things moving in the forest and out on the plains. It looks as if the faeries who have not joined us have conveniently disappeared."

Now that the fire had thinned out the forest, they could see across the lake to the White Tower—Liadan's tower. It made Roisin shudder to look at it. It rose from a wide base of rough-hewn caves, getting narrower and more complicated and intricate as it climbed. Towers shot from the top of it in all directions like frozen fireworks. It was as if someone had started to build their dream castle and then turned it into a nightmare, cramming it with every possible feature, from overblown ornate plastering to hopelessly frilly balconies edging top windows, until it became grotesque with its own fancies.

"**You are dismissed**," the Morrighan said to the scout. He bowed his head and turned his horse's head to work his way through the ranks.

Aengus Óg nudged his horse forward. "What is Cernunnos playing at?" he asked. "Does he mean to hold out in the White Tower until winter comes and his wife's power grows stronger?"

"No, that is not his way," said the Morrighan. "Cernunnos never had time for sieges—he thought they were a coward's way of waging war."

"Then where is he?" asked Nuada.

"He always was cunning in battle," said Meabh, spurring her horse forward to join Aengus Óg. "He's leading us into a bottleneck." She pointed to the narrow road that led from the beach around the hill where the tower squatted, weaving around and around like a dusty ribbon until it reached the bronze gates of the tower, flashing in the sun.

"I see his plan," said the Morrighan. "He hopes to put us in such a position that our greater numbers will be no advantage at all."

"Well, I don't see it," said Niamh petulantly, while Sorcha sighed and rolled her eyes.

"Look, bubblehead," said Meabh, pointing to the road that wound up to the tower gates. "See how wide that road is?" Niamh nodded. "How many soldiers do you think can travel abreast there?"

Niamh frowned. "Two?"

"Exactly," said Meabh. "Liadan and Cernunnos can hold off this great army at the gates of the White Tower with just a handful of men, because they only need to fight us two at a time. Our troops will have to line up on the road and wait their turn to do battle, while Liadan's elves pick us off, two by two. We could lose half our army just trying to breach the gates, and it will take weeks."

"But you can make sure this doesn't happen, can you not, Great Queen?" asked Sorcha. "With your help, we can take this advantage away."

"**Indeed**," said the Morrighan, nodding her veiled head. "**Do you and your men have something to protect your ears?**"

They all nodded. Roisin and Danny looked at each other and raised their eyebrows. "We don't," said Danny.

"That is hardly our concern," sneered Sorcha, while the Morrighan said nothing.

"**Meabh, ride on ahead and get us through the lake. It seems that the ice bridge has conveniently melted**," said the Morrighan. As Meabh went to ride past her, the Morrighan grabbed her arm. "**I'll be watching you, Meabh.**"

Meabh nodded and spurred her horse into a gallop. The Morrighan stood up in her stirrups and called to the army behind her. "**As soon as Queen Meabh clears a path, the cavalry will ride hell for leather and aim for the beach. Foot soldiers, I want you to run behind. Once we get to the beach your troops are to form ranks. Foot soldiers are to breach the road first, cavalry will follow behind. Once we reach the gates, we will take stock.**"

Roisin turned her head and saw the captains of the three courts nodding and passing the orders on to their seconds-in-command, who passed them on to the cavalry and so on, until the Morrighan's words rippled through the waiting ranks. She licked her lips nervously and sat deep in the saddle to get a better seat and took a tighter grip on her horse's reins. Danny whistled to get Nero's attention. "Be careful," he said.

The gray wolf nodded, his face tight with tension.

The world stood still as the assembled army watched Meabh gallop down to the stony beach. No wind blew across their faces or set banners snapping. There was not a sound from the assembled troops behind her. All eyes were focused on the red-haired figure as she slowed her horse to a walk. Meabh held up her hand and called out and the waters of the lake shot violently into the air. In front of Roisin's astonished eyes the towering wall of water hung suspended and then peeled itself in two, folding over and leaving a path clear from one beach to the other.

"**NOW**!" screamed the Morrighan, kicking her horse into a gallop. Every Tuatha horse surged forward at the same moment and Roisin clung to her horse's mane as the animal charged downhill toward the path, tipping Roisin forward and unbalancing her. Nero was a quicksilver streak ahead of the army, racing away from the lethal hoofs, throwing a lone shadow on the path still damp with lake water. Roisin's ears filled with the thunder of hoofs and her eyes teared in the wind, so she rode blind. She clung on until she thought her finger bones would snap and squeezed her eyes shut. She felt a coolness on her face and looked up to see the walls of water towering over her a mile high, fish still lazily swimming in their depths, unconcerned at the chasm that had just appeared in their world. On they galloped, the beach on the far side of the water tunnel shimmering in the summer sun.

She let out a sigh of relief when she heard her horse's hoofs crunch on the shale of the beach. The horse pulled up to a standing stop as the foot soldiers rushed past them and onto the road, disappearing out of sight around the first bend. When the last of the infantry were on the road the cavalry followed, with the monarchs, Roisin, Danny, Nero, and the precious casket at their heart.

Roisin found herself on the outside edge. She tried not to look down and see just how close her horse's hoofs were to the edge of the road and the long plunge to the rocks below. Her heart leaped into her throat when one of his hoofs slipped and part of the crust of the road tumbled into the lake below. She swallowed her scream and hid her face in his mane, trusting him to get her to the White Tower safely.

As they rounded the last corner and the road climbed in a fairly straight line to the ornate bronze gates of the tower, Roisin was horrified to hear shouts and screams. It seemed Cernunnos was more willing to join in battle than they had thought, and the gates had been opened to let loose the Winter Court's cavalry.

Liadan's elven mounts tore through the Tuatha foot soldiers like a blade through paper, raising their front legs to strike out with their talons, ripping the Tuatha who rushed to meet them. The mounts lashed out with their snake-like necks, sinking their fangs into the soldiers and flinging them off the road to their death. The elves on their backs stabbed with their long spears and the Tuatha found themselves being driven back. The mounts were packed close together and heavily armored, and with the long reach of their riders' weapons it was proving hard for the Tuatha to get close enough to inflict a mortal wound on mount or rider. The foot soldiers were slowly being driven back into the cavalry, falling off the side of the road as they collided with the mounted Tuatha behind them and found themselves with nowhere to put their feet.

Roisin screamed as her horse reared, lashing out with his front feet at the soldiers who pressed into him, infected by their panic.

"Great Queen, do something!" cried Nuada. "We cannot go back—there are too many behind us!"

The Morrighan reached up and pulled the veil from her face. Roisin gasped in horror as three faces fought and blurred across her skull—the young girl, the mother, the old woman, their mouths opening and closing like fishes' and their eyes rolling as they sought to be the dominant one. The Raven Queen stood up in her stirrups, launched herself into the air, and flew over the carnage, her shadow plunging the fighters below into darkness. Then she opened her mouth and the most horrible scream rolled out of her, a sonic boom that flattened Roisin's hair. It was filled with the sound of despair, so much so that Roisin began to weep and look at the cool blue waters of the lake below, actually tempted to throw herself into them. But the line held by the Winter Court's cavalry began to waver and then disintegrate as the Morrighan's shriek blasted at their ears and they turned and started to retreat up the road.

The Tuatha troops cheered and surged forward, and Roisin's horse shook his head to clear it of the Morrighan's scream and charged after them. They finally had a clear road to the gates, which were now hanging half off their hinges as the Tuatha soldiers pulled at them, their comrades flooding into the courtyard and up the wide stone steps that led to Liadan's hall. The carved wooden door with its intricate locks that guarded her inner hall had been smashed open.

Roisin dismounted with rubbery legs and wiped the tears from her eyes with the back of her hand. Danny rode up beside her, looking as if he was going to vomit. He got down and grabbed Roisin in a hug. "That was too close," he mumbled into her hair. She nodded and clutched at him, breathing in his warm smell and sending up a prayer of thanks that they were both still alive to whoever might be listening.

A heavy hand landed on their shoulders. The Morrighan pulled them up the stone steps with her, as soldiers hauled the casket from its cart and dragged it along behind them.

"**No time to celebrate, little ones**," said the Morrighan, her face veiled once again. "**The battle is not yet won.**"

chapter twenty-one

THE GREAT HALL OF THE WHITE TOWER WAS EMPTY
of its glittering court of elves and dark faeries. Liadan
sat on her throne of white-blue crystal at the end of the
chamber, her only attendant Cernunnos. The throne
sparkled in the light of the reflected summer sun, filter-
ing through arched windows to be caught and thrown
around the room by giant silver mirrors, so even in the
depths of the White Tower, the great hall shone with
light. Liadan had decided to face them wearing her tall
crown of ice, a cloak of heavy white fur around her shoulders, more white fur, and a sword at her feet. She glittered with diamonds and looked every inch the queen.
Her long black hair fell to her feet in shiny, glossy wings.

The Morrighan let go of Danny and Roisin and strode
over to Cernunnos.

"A sad day, brother," she said. "We must fix this wrong."

Cernunnos inclined his antlered head. "I was wrong to want peace all those years ago," he said. "The price was too high."

"Coward, that you desert me now," hissed Liadan as the sounds of looting and killing in the rest of the tower filtered through to them. Roisin closed her eyes at the noise of breaking glass, splintering wood, and screams cut short. "I am your queen, your wife. We swore loyalty to each other."

"Look at what that loyalty has cost me," said Cernunnos. "It was a mistake to ally with one who was not of my own kind. You have disappointed me. You have been faithless as a wife and are not fit to be a queen. You have destroyed the forest when I was not there to defend it. It was to protect the forest and the faeries who inhabited it that I married you in the first place. You were welcomed here when you needed sanctuary and bound with bonds of kinship to Tír na nÓg. You have broken them all—you are wife to me no longer."

"You married me only to please her!" Liadan spat, pointing at the Morrighan. "To keep her precious balance. The two of you are as blind as each other! *Power* is what matters—who wields it, how much they have. *Not balance.*"

"Where is Fenris?" said a voice by Roisin's hip. She looked down and realized that Nero had wound his way through the monarchs and their attendants to come stand by her side. "I can't see him."

Liadan smiled her cruel smile just as Danny took a closer look at the white fur at her feet. "NO!" he yelled. Nero howled and raced over, snuffling and nudging at it, whimpering when it wouldn't move. Roisin forced herself forward on numb legs and looked at it closely.

It was Fenris. His eyes were closed and a sword pierced his mouth. The black wolf had been blasted with such an intense cold it had iced his fur to white. She knelt down and ran a hand over his pelt, the petrified fur crackling and snapping off at her touch. His body still held a faint trace of warmth. A trail of blood led from his pierced mouth to a pillar a few feet away. Liadan's elves must have dragged him over to her while he was still breathing, as the Morrighan's army had stormed her gates. Dragged him, half conscious and in agony so the Winter Queen would not have to trouble herself to walk a few steps to kill him. She must have leaned down from her throne and placed her hands on his ribs and let the cold flow through her into him, stopping his heart and stilling his breath.

Roisin looked up at Cernunnos, his shadowed face unreadable beneath his antlers, his eyes two white points of light. Nero began to howl his grief into the vaulted ceiling.

"Why did you let her do this?" she asked, tears streaming down her face. "Fenris was a creature of the forest, you were his lord. He should have been able to look to you for protection."

"I was not here. I was at the gates," said Cernunnos.

"You shouldn't be here at all!" said Roisin. "You should have been protecting the forest and the dryads." She pointed at Fenris. "You should have been protecting *him*."

"Brother, this marriage has made you powerless," said the Morrighan. **"But this child has found a way to help you save face. You can still honor your sacred oaths of kinship and marriage. The crown can stay on Liadan's head and out of the grasp of the greedy Tuatha monarchs. If we do not keep balance then we will be standing here again in a few centuries, with more blood spilled. I can free you from your wife and give you honor again."**

Liadan cackled, a high, insane sound that looped around the room and competed with Nero's heartbroken howls. "You cannot kill me!" she said. "I am winter made flesh—how do you kill a season?"

The Morrighan turned her veiled face toward her. **"I will not have to."** She raised her voice. **"Bring it forward."**

The Tuatha soldiers dragged the casket to the foot of the dais and whipped the cloth from it. It gleamed in the light and all the Tuatha instinctively took a step back from its iron bindings.

The Morrighan bent her head toward Cernunnos. **"Let the child tell you a story and then you will see your way out of this."**

Roisin kept her eyes fixed on Liadan, proud and scornful on her throne. Roisin's hands still rested on Fenris's cold body as she started to speak.

"Once upon a time in midwinter, when snowflakes were falling like feathers from the sky, a queen sat sewing at her window and her embroidering frame was made of fine black ebony. As she was sewing and looking out at the snow, she pricked her finger with the needle and three drops of blood fell. The red looked so lovely against the white of the snow that she thought to herself, *I wish I had a child as white as snow, as red as blood, and as black as the ebony of my embroidering frame.*"

Liadan's eyes widened in horror and she half rose from her throne, bracing herself against its armrests as she shrieked, "NO! YOU CANNOT TOUCH ME! YOU CANNOT LAY HANDS ON ME!"

"I don't have to," said Roisin. "The story will do it all for me."

"I am a queen," hissed Liadan, stepping down from the throne, frost crackling out from her feet. "Who are you to challenge me, a grubby little mortal child who still cries when it thunders? You cannot imagine me away with your childish mortal tales. You cannot touch me; you cannot lay hands on a queen with all the cold of winter in her body."

"**But I can**," said the Morrighan. She pulled the veil from her face to reveal the wrinkly visage of the old woman and reached within her cloak to pull out the shiny, juicy red apple.

"Then a queen came, disguised as a hag, with a juicy red apple," continued Roisin, as the Morrighan grabbed Liadan's arm. "How Snow White, with her long black hair, her white skin, her red lips, longed to taste that apple."

Liadan screamed and raised her arms to fend the Morrighan off, her cold flaring and covering both their bodies in waves of ice. But the Morrighan ignored the bitter cold and shoved the apple into Liadan's open mouth, closing her long, black-tipped fingers over Liadan's lips. Liadan's teeth clamped down instinctively and her white eyes bulged, but it was too late—the flesh of the apple had already passed her lips and Liadan fell down in a faint at the Morrighan's feet, a chunk of apple lodged in her throat.

Roisin looked down at her body and her lip curled with contempt. "White as snow, red as blood, black as ebony. Give me your heart, dear Snow White."

She stood aside and watched as Tuatha, with their arms and hands armored against Liadan's cold, lifted her inert body and placed her inside the crystal casket, sealing the lid down tight.

"There she will stay, brother," said the Morrighan. "Let her hall crumble around her, let her name be forgotten. She will live and the crown will stay on her head. You have honored your vows as a husband—your wife is alive and safe, and none can call you an oath breaker."

No one thought to offer a word of comfort to poor Nero, who had ceased his howling and had curled up against his fallen pack leader. Roisin wept fresh tears as she watched him settle against Fenris's cold flank, swishing his tail over his nose and closing his eyes with a sigh. The Tuatha might have settled their affairs tidily, but there was to be no justice for the wolves of Tír na nÓg.

"Is that it?" demanded Sorcha. "Are we expected to just go home now?"

"**Yes**," said the Morrighan. "**You can divide up Liadan's possessions among yourselves as the spoils of war, but there will be no other advantage gained here.**"

The sound of wailing drifted faintly through the open doors at the end of the hall. Meabh's head shot up and she sniffed the air like a bloodhound. She and Niamh darted forward and seized Danny and Roisin. Nero leaped to his feet and snarled at them, his hackles rising. The Morrighan bent and put a warning hand on his neck.

"Perhaps not here, sweet sister," Meabh purred, "but there might be some advantage to be had in the mortal world. It seems our hopes of luring the Hound have been realized because, unless my ears deceive me, the mist of dreams is on the move. And if it's on the move, it means it's following the Hound. Let's give her what she came for, shall we?" Niamh giggled as they began to drag Danny and Roisin backward through the hall.

"What are you doing?" hissed Aengus Óg as Niamh went past.

"Thinking of myself, husband," she said. "As you did."

Some Tuatha moved forward as if they would stop Meabh and Niamh. Roisin felt her feet tripping over each other and she clawed at Meabh's arm, trying to get the Tuatha to loosen her grip and give her more room to breathe.

"**Stop**," said the Morrighan. "**Let them go.**" She looked at Meabh, her hag's face sour. "**Very well, Meabh. Let's see where this takes us.**"

"Oh, I know where it will be taking me," said Meabh as they reached the doors to the hall. "Straight into the mortal world and fresh territories."

chapter twenty-two

Roisin and Danny didn't fight this time as Niamh and Meabh dragged them down the steps of the great hall, calling for their troops still milling about in the courtyard to mount up and come with them. As Meabh threw her back into the saddle, all Roisin could think was, *Maddy is coming—Maddy is coming to bring us home!* Now, with Liadan imprisoned for the rest of her life, they could be free! They could go home and live normal lives, where the most important thing she had to worry about was math homework.

So she didn't sit there, inert, when Meabh and Niamh galloped from the courtyard, their soldiers flowing through the gates after them. She turned her horse's head, kicked her legs against his sides and yelled, "Giddyup!"

She raced out of the courtyard with Danny, their horses neck and neck, grinning wildly at each other through their horses' manes as the wind whipped them back into their faces. They thundered down the road toward the beach, whooping and cheering as their horses ran for the joy of it. It didn't matter what Meabh had planned—Maddy was coming! They were going home!

Maddy rode at the head of the mist of dreams, trying not to listen to the lunatic babble behind her as the split souls jabbered and screeched. She was sitting astride a fine black horse that Finn mac Cumhaill had loaned to her, but the animal was skittish at the noise. She leaned down and put a hand on his neck to soothe him as he pranced and snorted. She could see the mound now, looming on her left, its shadow defying all laws of nature to lie around it. The curve of the river bent away from it to flow past her, and on her right was the wounded forest of Tír na nÓg. She hoped that the mist was alerting every faerie creature that it was on the move. She had no way of knowing that Meabh knew what she was doing. But Maddy knew that if she did, she would come running. She only hoped that she brought Danny, Roisin, and Nero with her. Behind her, hidden in the depths of the mist, were two hundred Fianna, armed with long shields and pikes. *Please let this work,* she thought. *Please, please, let this work.*

The twin walls of water were still up as they headed for the beach. Meabh spurred her horse on with kicks and wild yells, and even though Roisin knew the poor animal must be exhausted, it still found a burst of speed from somewhere. She leaned away from her mount to help it keep its balance as it took the corner, crashed down from the beach on to the lake bed, and ran after Meabh. Roisin eyed the walls of water nervously, terrified that at any moment the spell Meabh had put on them would fail and they would come crashing down on their heads, drowning them all in a roar of waves. But they held, and she breathed a sigh of relief as her horse began to scramble up the far side and into the forest. She coughed as clouds of ash blew up from the impact of his hoofs and her eyes streamed red, but still her horse ran on and her heart sang.

Almost the moment they left the forest, Meabh and Niamh yanked back hard on their horses' reins, the animals' mouths gaping wide as the bits yanked their jaws down. They shuddered to an immediate halt, their hindquarters bunching underneath them, throwing up a shower of dirt as their hoofs plowed through the ground to bring them to a standstill.

Danny stood up in his stirrups and peered over Meabh's head. "There she is! Roisin, I can see her!" The closest Tuatha soldier turned and slapped him hard across his face, splitting his lip. Roisin sidled her horse closer, leaned over, and gripped his hand hard. "We're going home!" she whispered. Danny nodded at her, still smiling as he blotted the blood on his mouth with the back of his hand.

"So, Hound," cried Meabh, "you came after all. Are you ready to give me what I want in return for your family?"

"You must be as crazy as Liadan, Meabh," Maddy called back. "I told you before. I'm never going to give you what you want. I'm never going to be the kind of Hound you want."

Danny and Roisin looked at each other, confused. "What's she doing?" whispered Danny. Roisin shrugged, but her excitement was rapidly souring, turning into fear. She hoped Maddy had a plan and wasn't just mouthing off. Though she really couldn't trust Maddy *not* to be mouthing off.

"There is still time to change that," snarled Meabh.

Something made Roisin look over her shoulder and she could see a line of dust moving down the road from the White Tower. Someone was coming after them. Meabh might not have as much time as she thought.

"Yeah?" called Maddy. "Well, come on over here and try, if you think you're hard enough!"

That was the final straw. "Get her!" screamed Niamh to her soldiers. "Bring her to me. Let's cut the little pup open and see how brave she is then!"

Roisin's heart sank as she saw Niamh and Meabh's cavalry form a line and then charge straight at Maddy.

Maddy gripped her reins tight and watched the cavalry charge toward her, the pounding of their horses' gigantic hoofs shaking the ground as they came. Her own horse threw his head up and whinnied in fear. She stroked the long line of his satin neck and whispered, "Steady, steady," in a soft low voice, trying to give the animal confidence she didn't feel. She licked her lips nervously and watched the mist begin to spread through the trees on her right-hand side, outflanking the Tuatha who were getting closer with every beat of her heart.

Wait until you see the whites of their eyes, Finn mac Cumhaill had said. *Hold your nerve, hold the line, and don't move a muscle until you can see the whites of their eyes.*

Sweat trickled down her back and Maddy's breath whistled from between clenched teeth as she tried to stay calm and trust Finn's advice. Her horse began to sidle backward, wrenching his head to the side, trying to force her to let him run as the Tuatha got closer, and it took nearly all her concentration to keep him under control.

Nearly all. She still watched for the whites of their eyes, and as soon as she saw them she screamed, "NOW!"

The Fianna ran forward from the mist and formed a line in front of her, shielding themselves as they did so. Each man planted the butt of his pike on the ground, the wicked spears pointing straight at the chests of the first line of the Tuatha horses.

As soon as the Tuatha saw what was waiting for them they tried to pull their horses to a halt, but it was too late. The great beasts had no time to stop, and even though their riders pulled their heads up, momentum carried them forward onto the blades of the pikes. Maddy closed her eyes as the beasts screamed, falling back onto their riders and pulling the pikes from the hands of the Fianna. The horses roared in pain and thrashed on bloody ground as the pikes impaled in their chests whipped and bounced with their every move, striking their riders as they tried to get to their feet and draw their swords. Some Tuatha lay crushed and still beneath their writhing mounts. The Fianna drew the long swords belted at their waists and rushed to attack the Tuatha, screaming a war cry as they went. Maddy gathered up her reins and urged her horse forward, over the line of crushed bodies.

❧

Roisin cringed as she heard the crump of the Tuatha horses colliding with the shield wall. Danny looked at her, his mouth a round *O* of horror as the horses started to scream. "She's got a plan," he said. "That's got to be a good thing, right?"

"If it gets us out of here alive, yeah," said Roisin, watching as Niamh prepared to send a second wave of riders into the battle to cut down the Fianna on the ground.

"How confident are we feeling about that, on a scale of one to ten?" asked Danny.

Roisin watched as Meabh held her hand up just before Niamh's warriors charged. "Wait!" Meabh said, watching the mist as it crept alongside them. "Where is Finn mac Cumhaill?"

A second later, she got her answer. Finn mac Cumhaill and the rest of his men came riding out of the mist with swords drawn, their faces grim and silent. Their horses moved like ghosts, their hoofs wrapped in cloth to keep them silent. The Tuatha warriors didn't have time to turn their horses to face this new threat, and Finn mac Cumhaill's troops charged straight into their sides, hacking and stabbing. Meabh immediately sent a whirlwind of air about her body, driving the Fianna back, while Niamh threw back her cloak and her body pulsed with a solar flare.

Blinded, Roisin screamed, dropped her reins, and clapped her hands over her eyes. Seconds later she felt hands tugging at her and she hit out at the person who was trying to pull her from the saddle.

"Roisin, it's OK, it's me!" said a familiar voice.

"Maddy?" she asked, just before she was torn from the saddle and flung to the ground, all the breath driven from her body. She climbed stiffly to her feet, blinking frantically, spots dancing in front of her eyes. She could barely see, only dim shapes. A thud and a yelp nearby told her Maddy had managed to get Danny down from the saddle as well.

Maddy grabbed them both by the arm and began to pull them up the hill toward the mound. "Come on, we've got to get out of here," she panted. "Where's Nero?"

"We had to leave him behind," said Danny. "They grabbed us so fast I don't think he could catch up to us."

"Liadan killed Fenris, Maddy," said Roisin. "We were too late."

Maddy clenched her teeth. "Then there's nothing we can do. Just keep moving."

She managed to get them both to the entrance of the mound. Their eyes were red and swimming with tears and they kept looking at her ears rather than at her. They still couldn't see properly. *Maybe that was a good thing,* thought Maddy. They couldn't see the Morrighan and the rest of the Tuatha gathering at the foot of hill, by the bend in the river. They couldn't see the Fianna, fleeing to the boats they had waiting for them downriver, the horsemen galloping into the distance now that their job was done. The mist was creeping up the hill toward them. She had to get them out of here.

"I need you to step into the mound and walk quickly until you reach the mortal side," she said. "Put your hands on the walls and feel your way along. Apart from the central chamber, it's a straight run. You can do it. The mist of dreams is going to fill the mound behind you. It makes weird noises, but you've heard it before so just keep going. Don't stop, don't look back, don't try to turn back."

"You make it sound like you're not coming with us," said Danny, his voice tense. His hands reached out and gathered up handfuls of her hoodie and gripped her hard.

"I'm not," said Maddy gently, trying to untangle his fingers. "I'm going to stay here and finish this."

"You don't have to do that!" said Roisin. "We got Liadan—she's never going to come after you again."

"It's about more than Liadan," said Maddy. "I realize now, she's small fry compared to the Tuatha. They are the ones I have to stop. I used to be so scared of Liadan, but now I see she's just an irritant. The mist will go a long way to locking the mound, but I don't think it's enough."

"You can't kill them," said Danny.

"No, but I can give them a kicking that will leave them licking their wounds for a long time to come," said Maddy.

"This isn't your job," said Danny, his face grim. "You're coming back with us." He gripped her hard again, and this time Roisin leaned forward and grabbed a handful of her clothing as well.

But right at that moment the mist began to gather around them as it funneled into the mound. The split souls chattered and jabbered with excitement and some took shape for a moment, arms and hands snaking out of the mist to pry Danny and Roisin's fingers off Maddy and to push the siblings ahead of the mist, deep into the mound.

"Thank you," Maddy said. Hands reached down and patted her face and stroked her hair as the mist flowed over her.

"Maddy . . . !" she heard Roisin wail from deep inside the mound. "Please come with us before it's too late. We love you!"

She sobbed at that and her knees almost buckled as she pressed the back of her hand to her eyes. "I love you too, both of you," she called into the mound, her voice breaking. "Tell Granny and Granda I will miss them and I love them."

There was one last, desperate wail from Roisin that faded away, and then the dregs of the mist were sucked into the mound. She watched as the mound sealed itself up and she was faced with a grassy bank, solid and innocent as the hill it stood on.

She tipped her head back to stop the tears from spilling down her face and looked up at the sky. The sun was going down and the clouds were a fluffy baby pink. This world, this mirror image of the mortal one she would never see again, was so beautiful it made her throat ache. *This is it*, she thought. *I will never get to grow up.* She thought wistfully of beautiful, witty Kitty. *I would have liked to have danced like her, in a pretty dress. Just once.*

She braced herself to turn and face the Tuatha when a punch to her shoulder sent her sprawling face down in front of the mound. She winced, and when she opened her eyes a pair of dirty gray feet with black toenails were level with her nose. She looked up at Una. "That really hurt," she said.

"Well, an arrow in the shoulder will do that to you," said Una. "Give it ten minutes and it's *really* going to hurt."

"Do you think I have ten minutes?" said Maddy.

Una looked over Maddy's head and wrinkled her nose. "Probably not."

Maddy raised her hand. "Here, help me up, will you?"

She sobbed with pain as Una tried to pull her to her feet as gently as she could and then she turned to face the Morrighan.

What was left of the Tuatha army was ranged against her at the bottom of the hill, the bend of the river marking their boundary. The last of the Fianna were fleeing back toward the Shadowlands, and Maddy was relieved the Tuatha were letting them go. All their attention was focused on her, which was exactly what she wanted. The monarchs looked sullen and angry, all except Nuada, Sorcha's husband, who had a satisfied smile on his face and a bow in his hand. Maddy guessed he was the one who had shot her. Cernunnos and the Morrighan were unreadable, as usual. The Morrighan's veil was back over her face.

"**I should have put you down when I had the chance,**" she hissed. "**Hounds are nothing but trouble. Too many Tuatha have died today because of you. And now you think fit to break the treaty. We were given one night a year, and one night we shall have.**"

"Not anymore," said Maddy, swaying on her feet as the pain in her shoulder worsened.

"**Do you really think that mist will stop us?**" sneered the Morrighan.

"It stopped you from walking through a fair bit of what you called your territory," said Maddy. "So, yes, I think it will stop you from getting through one doorway. But it's not like that's all I've got planned for you."

"**Pray tell**," said the Morrighan.

"I know what the Hounds have always known," said Maddy. "I've figured out how this place works. All these years you've been telling people that you are all-powerful, our natural masters, our gods. The truth is, you need us more than we need you. In fact, you're pretty disposable as far as humans are concerned."

The Tuatha began to mutter among themselves, but the Morrighan gave nothing away. "**You have no idea what you are talking about, child**," she said.

"I think I do," said Maddy. "Our imaginations make us pretty amazing. Since you were banished beneath the mounds we've grown as a species in so many ways. Yet you've stayed exactly the same. As a race, you know all you are ever going to know. That's why you lost the war in the first place, despite your powers—you could never outthink us. Now look at you, stuck underground, needing human imaginations to keep your world going, to keep you fed. And you still can't control it.

"The truth is, this place is ours," Maddy went on. "Roisin showed me that. With enough imagination, a human can make this place do pretty much whatever they want. Watch this." Maddy waved her hand at the water in the river and it rushed away, leaving a pebbled bed bare beneath the evening sun and a few fish flopping on the stones as they gasped for air.

"Isn't that amazing?" said Maddy, smiling with mock innocence as the Tuatha began to panic and mutter among themselves. "But you did find our biggest weakness. We humans always have to believe in something bigger than ourselves; we've always needed gods for comfort. You exploited that."

"**Archers!**" called the Morrighan. A group of Tuatha ran up behind the monarchs and began to notch silver-tipped arrows into bows. Maddy felt her stomach clench. *I have to do it now.*

"But if I want to have a god, I can pick whoever I like in here—it doesn't have to be you all," she said, as the ground began to rumble beneath her feet.

The Tuatha cried out in panic and looked upstream, where a huge wall of water was bearing down on them as the river rushed to fill its natural place.

"**Archers, take aim,**" said the Morrighan.

"Here's one I quite like the look of!" yelled Maddy over the sound of the tsunami. "Poseidon, god of the sea and horses, thunder roarer, earth shaker!"

The Tuatha screamed as the wall of water loomed above them, casting a shadow before it. The foam at its crest writhed and turned into horses, but they didn't stay white. They turned black, as black as night, and their red eyes burned with rage as the wave began to fall.

"See, Meabh?" screamed Maddy over the roar of the water as the Autumn Queen looked at her in terror. "There's your hate, there's your rage! I HOPE YOU CHOKE ON IT!"

"FIRE!" screamed the Morrighan as the archers loosed their bows. A deadly cloud of arrows arced through the air and then began to fall toward Maddy, singing as they came. She spread her arms wide to welcome them as the wave collapsed and the black horses raced on. Just before it went dark, she thought, *Why isn't Una singing?*

EPILOGUE

GRANDA SAT BY THE FIRE AND LISTENED TO THE rain gust at the window. It was a light and fragile spray, a soft autumn rain that would only mist against the skin. The wind sighed gently around the little cottage, the season too early to give it the strength to howl. George, the little black-and-white terrier, lay in front of the fire. His muzzle was nearly completely gray now, and when Granda stood up and walked across the room, the little dog merely lifted his sad brown eyes to follow him. He didn't have the energy to jump up and run after him anymore.

Granda walked quietly to the door of his bedroom and cracked it open slightly. He could hear his wife's deep, even breathing and see the bottle of pills that sat on her bedside table. Three months on, and she was still taking pills to help her sleep, to stop her from roaming the house or sitting in Maddy's bedroom, crying.

He did that for her now.

Granda closed the door gently. His shoulders slumped and he aged twenty years in two seconds as he opened a door to another bedroom. He sat down on the bed and smoothed the quilt with one gnarled hand and let a tear trickle through the gray stubble on his face.

Maddy wouldn't recognize the room now. The heavy dark-brown furniture was still there—their pensions couldn't stretch to getting it replaced—but the shiny embossed wallpaper Maddy had hated so much was gone. The walls were stripped back to the plaster and painted a pale pink and the bed linen he sat on was striped in pink and green. Everything Maddy owned had been unpacked and displayed neatly on shelves. The room was full of her life: her photographs in frames showing her parents and her friends in London, laughing, her books, her worn teddy bear, the trinkets she had taken a shine to. Scatter cushions were propped up against plump pillows and Fionnula had even paid for a leather barrel-back chair and pretty Venetian mirror. It was the perfect girl's room.

"She'll like it, won't she, Bat?" Granny had asked, twisting a hanky between her hands, tears making tracks on her cheeks as they flowed silently and relentlessly. "Isn't it just what she always wanted?" It was as if she hoped that the perfect bedroom would be a siren call to the missing child, that Maddy would walk back through the door and lay her head down on the pillow, a smile on her lips.

Granda wasn't sure that they had ever really known what Maddy had wanted, but he had told his wife that the room she had worked so hard on was beautiful, that when Maddy came home she would love it. That she would stay this time and she would be happy, just as her mother once had been. And then he guided his wife out with a hand on her elbow, her fingers still strangling her handkerchief, helped her into their bed, and poured her a glass of water for her pills. He sat and watched while she drifted into sleep, her face still creased by grief.

He touched his face and wondered what he looked like. He remembered how Danny and Roisin had looked, their eyes red and teary from the solar flare as they had stumbled from the mound, sobbing that Maddy was gone, that the mound was locked, that there was no way to reach her. Although their eyes had healed, the haunted look never left them. Even Fionnula's face was marked with guilt. *What had Maddy's face looked like,* he wondered, *as she faced the Tuatha? Had they run her to ground, crouched and sobbing, her back to the mound, or had she stood and faced them?* He smiled. He was willing to bet everything he had that his granddaughter had stood straight and proud at the end.

He got up and closed the door on that perfect room, a room that was cleaned and aired every week, ready for a girl who could not find her way home. As the fire snapped and popped in the grate, Granda took his coat down from a hook by the door, wound a black wool scarf around his neck, and pulled a flat cap onto his head. George looked up and wagged his tail half-heartedly as his ears caught the jangle of keys.

"Stay," said Granda sternly.

The dog sighed and dropped his head back down onto his paws.

Granda stepped out into the autumn night and eased the door shut behind him. He thrust his gloveless hands into the deep pockets of his coat and walked up the road, in the direction of the castle. As the rain blurred his eyes he thought about what could have happened to Maddy.

Perhaps Danny and Roisin were right. Perhaps Maddy had died on the other side of the mound. They had tried to go back in after her, but the mist of dreams wouldn't let them pass. The split souls were loyal to the Hound and would not break Maddy's rule that no one passed through them, not even Maddy's blood.

Or would they? *Something* had crept from the mound in the three months since it had been sealed. Something had got through, some creature that made the Sighted's collective hairs stand on end, but it wasn't a faerie. It was a dark thing that roamed the night and haunted dreams and made babies whimper in their sleep. Villagers locked their doors against it, but for different reasons. The Sighted were terrified that the creature belonged to the Tuatha and that it had come to seek revenge for what Maddy had done. The Unsighted locked their doors and windows because locking the night out eased that nameless dread. He had done it too, sick and sore as he was in grief, in fear that he would lose another loved one, another grandchild, or perhaps his wife to the thing that stalked the lanes and roads around Blarney.

But it was only when little Stephen Forest was found crying and confused in the middle of the road, half asleep in his pajamas, claiming he had seen Maddy, that Granda had begun to wonder. The child's mother had shushed the boy and hurried him away, fearful of adding to her neighbors' grief. But no one knew better than Bat that only children tell you what they *know* they have seen, not what they *think* they have seen.

So here he was in the dead of night, walking toward that cursed castle, with only an iron cuff on his wrist to protect him if something went wrong. His heart hammered in his chest and he had to concentrate hard to slow his breathing. His steps rang out, rebounding off the stone wall on his right to bounce and echo across the square. He kept his eyes fixed on the end of the lane, where it spread into the parking lot of the castle. As he watched, something stepped from the shadows.

It was a huge black horse, with burning red eyes. The asphalt of the road bubbled beneath its hoofs and steam curled from its flared nostrils. Its rider was small and cloaked from head to foot in black, its face hidden in the dark. It urged the horse on toward Granda at a walk and the rider hissed when he stopped dead. The two of them stood there, facing each other, while the horse fidgeted and steamed in the cool autumn air.

"Danny and Roisin told me the things that were said to you beneath the mound," said Granda. "They told me about the poison Meabh poured into your ears, what she tried to turn you into. I think she'd be happy if she saw you now, Maddy."

The rider hissed again and the horse took another step forward, but Granda squared his shoulders and held his ground.

"If you hadn't run off so quick, Maddy, you could have talked to me about what being the Hound meant," he said. "Meabh was only ever going to tell you what it suited her to have you believe. I never got the chance to tell you what the Hound really is. The Hound is loyal, loving, enduring, steadfast, and true. You are the best of us, Maddy. Only the very best mortal, with the most human heart, gets the job of standing vigil on a watch that lasts their whole life. That's why I know you can't hurt me. You're the best of me and I love you, Maddy, more than I love myself. And you are still capable of love, even after everything you have been through. You are a Hound that would make Cú Chulainn weep with shame."

His words caught in his throat as the rider kicked the horse forward and it bore down on him at a steady canter. "I *know* you could never hurt me, dear," and he put his arms up as the horse collided with him and then passed through him, freezing his heart in his chest as it went, a cold breath of despair. But still he reached up and his warm hands found a child's thin arms and he pulled the rider close to him, the two of them tumbling to the ground. As the horse screamed with rage and began to drift apart on the air, he hugged that thin body close to him and pulled the hood back from its head. The black cloth disintegrated beneath his fingers, no more substantial than a spider's web. Now there were soft brown curls under his fingers and a small white face, the ridge of a scar marring one cheek. The cloak faded away to reveal grubby blue jeans, a torn hoody, scuffed sneakers. But he didn't see any of that, because he couldn't stop looking into the glass-green eyes that stared up at him, wide and confused, filling up with rain and tears. Long fingers clutched at his collar as her mouth gasped and he kissed those fingers, hugging her close and sobbing with relief as Maddy's eyes closed and she slipped into unconsciousness.

⟳

Sleep closed her eyes and stopped her ears, sucking her down into blue velvet coils. She lay cocooned in clean linen, which smelled of sunshine, her body wrapped in a thick duvet, her head burrowing into a feather pillow and a mattress that swallowed every angle of her bones until she drifted, weightless. There were no dreams anymore, no voices jabbering at her, shredding her peace with sharp words. The rooms in her mind were locked and she knew she would return to them only if she wanted to. Now and then her lids eased open and she was aware of bright lights and worried faces. Sometimes people talked to her, but she didn't know if she talked back. Once, her body had been lifted out of its warm cocoon and soft white bread had been laid on her tongue, and salty soup. But it was too easy to drift back into that still, quiet place that cuddled her close.

It couldn't last. She felt the coils loosen and slip away, pushing her forward, forcing her from the deep velvet blue and back toward cold air, sharp edges, and a kaleidoscope of colors. Her eyes opened in her room in Blarney.

She sat up, confused, and switched the light on beside her bed. Except it didn't look like her bed. The old-lady look was gone, replaced by pink-and-green girlishness. It was very strange to see her things in this setting. She swung her legs out of bed and found a pair of jeans and a sweater folded neatly on a leather chair she had never seen before. She pulled the jeans on, and as she straightened up she staggered and put a hand out against the chest of drawers to stop herself from falling. There was a flash of movement from the corner of her eye and she snapped her head around to face the wild-eyed creature that was staring at her. It took her a couple of seconds to realize that the gaunt, scarred girl was her reflection in an ornate mirror.

She opened the door that divided her bedroom from the living room in the little cottage and saw Granda sitting by the fire. He smiled as he looked up at her. The curtains were drawn and the room was dark. She looked at the clock on the mantelpiece above the fire. Three in the morning. She wondered how she looked to him, her clothes hanging off her emaciated frame, the red puckered scar that ran down one cheek, her wild, matted hair standing on end.

"You're awake at last," he said.

"How long have I been asleep?"

"A few days," he said. "You looked as if you needed it."

She said nothing and walked across to the fire, sitting down cross-legged in front of it. She gazed into its red heart until her face began to burn and she turned her cheek to it, shaking her hair over it as a barrier. She looked at Granda.

"My room is very . . . pink."

He laughed softly. "Your granny decorated it for you."

"How is she?"

"She was bad, for a while," said Granda. "But overjoyed you are home. She's been sitting with you for days. I made her go to bed tonight. She'll be raging she wasn't awake when you woke up."

Maddy smiled and looked back at the fire. "It's going to take a lot of explaining, me coming back."

"The Sighted will find a way," said Granda.

"Yes, you always do, don't you?" said Maddy, a trace of her old bitterness creeping back into her voice. She sat and thought for a couple of minutes and then said. "Are they gone?"

Granda sighed. "The Tuatha? Probably not. They haven't been seen above the mound since Danny and Roisin came back, and from the sound of things you dealt them quite a blow. But they are hard to kill, and the Seeing Stones sustain them. I'd say they are still beneath us, biding their time."

"You know what I did then?"

Granda nodded. "Danny and Roisin told us some of it, and you told us the rest during one of your more lucid moments."

"How did I get back?"

"Who knows?" said Granda. "It seems you were able to get on the back of one of those horses you conjured up and perhaps the force of the wave swept you through the mound. Perhaps the split souls will let the Hound, out of all the mortals and the faeries, come and go as she pleases, but I would rather we didn't test that theory out. The important thing is that you are back."

"How did you know it was me?"

"I didn't. But I knew you weren't dead."

"How?"

"Una didn't keen," said Granda. "If you had died in front of the mound in Tír na nÓg, Una would have sung for you, and the Sighted and the faeries would have heard it, wherever we were. But she was silent, so I knew you were still alive. Who else could have come out of the mound after Danny and Roisin?"

Maddy smiled. "Where is Una?"

"She hasn't been seen for months," said Granda. "We thought she was tracking you, staying close to you."

Maddy frowned and fell silent again. The clock ticked away the seconds. The fire collapsed in a little heap and flared crimson.

"They're going to come for me again, aren't they?" she asked, her voice hard and brittle.

Granda sighed. "Who knows, Maddy? Maybe what you have done will keep them away for the rest of your life. I think they will find a way through eventually." He leaned down and cupped her chin in his hand, forcing her to look up at him. "But if they do come for you again, Maddy, you'll be bigger and stronger. As you grow up, all the monsters in your life will get smaller and smaller. Even them. They know that too. Small as you are, Maddy, you gave them a bad bite. They won't forget that in a hurry."

They smiled at each other, Maddy dashing away tears with the back of her hand. "Go to bed, love," said Granda. "You're exhausted and you need more rest."

"In a minute," said Maddy. "I'd like to get a bit of fresh air."

"Five minutes," said Granda. "And then I'm putting you back to bed."

"Five minutes," agreed Maddy.

She slipped out into the backyard, shivering in the cold air, the gravel of the garden path cutting into the soles of her bare feet. She looked up at the stars and dragged in lungfuls of crisp air. A movement by the gate caught her eye and she smiled as a little gray figure shuffled into view.

"Una," she said. "You got through the mound!"

Una snorted with contempt. "Barely. Those split souls howled loud enough to make my ears bleed, but if they can't stop the Hound, they can't stop one who is bound by oath and magic to follow her. But I would appreciate it, girl, if you didn't make me do that again anytime soon."

Maddy grinned. "Then you'll be pleased to hear I won't be going anywhere for quite some time."

"Good!" said Una. She stood next to Maddy and they looked at the stars together. Maddy wiggled her toes, which were beginning to go numb, and marveled at every move her body made, every twitch of muscle, the pulse of the blood running through her veins and the breath pulling in and out of her chest. She was alive. For the first time since her parents had died, years stretched ahead of Maddy that were golden with promise, a far horizon that was drenched with sunshine. She stood there, shivering, as the bright stars wheeled above her head and promised herself that she was going to enjoy every single second of her future and she wouldn't let a day go by she didn't tell the people she cared for that she loved them. Starting now.

She bent down and hugged Una hard, breathing in the smell of damp earth that always seemed to cling to the banshee's rags. "Thank you for watching over me," Maddy said. "I love you, Una."

"That's nice," said the little faerie woman, patting her awkwardly on the shoulder. "But they do say actions speak louder than words. Any Cheese & Onion crisps for the road?"

Maddy laughed and let go of the banshee, stepping back and leading her into the warm glow of the kitchen, where Granny was waiting, with tears pouring down her face and into the curve of her smile, to sweep Maddy into her arms.

HOW TO SAY THE CHARACTERS' NAMES

Aengus Óg	*ain*-gus ohg
Cú Chulainn	coo cullen
Fachtna	*foct*-na
Fianna	fee-anna
Finn mac Cumhaill	fin mac cool
Fionnula	fin-*oo*-la
Hy Breasail	high brazil
Meabh	mayv
Niamh	*nee*-iv
Nuada	*noo*-i-da
Roisin	*roe*-sheen
Sorcha	*sor*-ka
Una	*oo*na

Exploring the
Faerie Realm

The Raven Queen draws on Irish myth and legend to create a magical world. Read on to find out more about these ancient stories . . .

Banshees—Banshees follow the great families of Ireland and all their descendants and wail just before their deaths as a warning, and also afterward, so that the world will know someone with hero's blood has passed. Whether they are supposed to act as guardian angels for the families or whether Una simply decided to take this task upon herself, no one is really sure. But I think it's safe to say that having a Cheese & Onion Tayto–munching banshee looking out for you is not normal.

Cernunnos (ker-*noo*-nos)—One of the oldest and most powerful of the TUATHA DE DANNAN, he clings to the form he took when he was worshipped in pre-Christian Ireland, the horned god. But he likes to linger in our world too, so he takes on human form for the winter months, calls himself Seamus ("*shay*-mus") and lives in Blarney, County Cork, keeping an eye on the mortal world and any coming and goings from TÍR NA NÓG. It's a weird way to spend your vacations, but who's going to argue with an ancient Celtic god?

The Coranied (kor-a-need)—Thousands of years ago, the Coranied, a mysterious race of warlocks, lived in Ireland and imprisoned the Celts. When the Celts rose up against the TUATHA, the Coranied followed them beneath the mounds. They have a unique talent—they can harvest all the bad thoughts and dreams that people have, which is what the dark faeries need for nourishment. THE MORRIGHAN protects the Coranied in return for this talent and she rations the dark faeries, keeping them too weak to wage war. The Coranied are vital to the Morrighan to keep balance in TÍR NA NÓG. In turn, they are completely loyal to the Morrighan and think only of how to keep the balance. They care for no one and nothing outside of this.

Liadan (*lee*-ah-dan)—Means "gray lady" in Irish. Liadan is an old and powerful elf from the Nordic countries. No one knows why she and her clan came to TÍR NA NÓG seeking sanctuary, but she's as argumentative as the TUATHA DE DANNAN. Do you know someone in school who could start a fight in an empty room? That's Liadan. The only good thing about her is that she unites the Tuatha against her. Everyone needs someone to hate, right?

The Morrighan (more-*ee*-gan)—In pre-Christian Ireland, the Morrighan was worshipped as a triple-faced goddess. She represents the maiden, the mother, and the hag and is the most powerful of the Tuatha de Dannan. She speaks with a triple voice and it is her power that created Tír na nóg and her power alone that maintains the boundaries between faerie and mortal worlds. The Morrighan is one of the most dangerous of the Tuatha. She is also known as the Raven Queen and is the living embodiment of war. Waking the Morrighan is not something that should be done lightly.

Pooka—The Pooka is a malicious faerie that appears in many guises all over Ireland, as a goat, a horse, or a dog, always jet-black with yellow eyes. Some say he is a harbinger of death, others that he is just a nuisance that terrorizes travelers up on the road at night. As Meabh's familiar, he always appears as a huge black dog.

Tír na nóg (teer na nogue)—The Land of Eternal Youth. The fabled realm of the TUATHA DE DANNAN that exists beneath Ireland's surface, the place they fled to when they lost their battles against mortals for control of Ireland. This is where the Tuatha and the lesser tribes of faeries live. Many, many people search for ways in, but you need a faerie guide to enter the realm, and getting out is never as easy. Something to think about if you have things urgent to do topside—I'd clear your diary.

Tuatha de Dannan (*too*-ay day *dah*-nan)—The Tuatha have many names: the Shining Ones, the Fair Folk, the Gentry. Some call them faeries, but they call themselves gods. They used to be in charge of Ireland, until St. Patrick came along, and they have serious powers. They can control all the elements (air, water, fire, and earth), cast powerful spells, and change their form at will. They are vain and short-tempered, cruel, and spiteful. They argue so much that fighting has practically become a hobby. They are the most powerful beings in TÍR NA NÓG, and they rule it. It's best not to upset them.

Acknowledgments

Writers always get the sole credit for putting a book together, but there is a huge team behind any book that helps bring it to life. I can't thank everybody who has touched the Blarney Trilogy, but a few people do stand out. First is Laura Cecil, my agent. Everything I write starts its journey with her. She tells me if it's going to work, holds my hand if I think it is so bad my career will spiral down the drain as a result, and gives me advice, which is always spot on, whether I like it or not. Niamh Mulvey has worked on all three books and has taken charge of editing the last two. As a fluent Irish speaker she is invaluable for pointing out misspellings and abuse of the language in the two books as well as being happy to spend hours discussing the finer points of plot. Thanks for leaving all the blood and gore in, Niamh! Then there is Talya Baker, who has copyedited all three. Myself and Niamh spend days trying to turn out perfect copy so we can catch Talya out, but she always manages to find at least six mistakes on every page. But it is thanks to Talya that the books are perfect in terms of grammar and spelling, so much easier to read. She also catches all those tiny little details that don't make sense because of the cack-handed way I have written them, so each book flows smoothly. Last but not least there is my Facebook network of fellow writers, librarians, and readers, who keep me going day to day with funny GIFs and encouraging messages about how much they, or someone they know, like Maddy. Or Fachtna. Who knew a homicidal faerie would be such a hit?

About the Type

Typeset in Utopia Regular, 10/14.25 pt.

Utopia is a multifunctional typeface designed by Robert Slimbach in 1989. It is solidly based on types of the eighteenth century, with the addition of contemporary type innovations.

Typeset by Scribe Inc., Philadelphia, Pennsylvania